NO MORE GAMES

DAVE BARRETT

For all those who could have given up on me at some point along the way, but didn't.

THE STORY THUS FAR

It's All Fun and Games

TJ Keller invited his best friend, Allison Duggan, to join him and his gaming friends for a weekend of Live Action Role Playing, and she reluctantly said yes. Though new to the activity, Allison jumped right in, agreeing to be the party's healer as they set off on their quest to confront the power-mad wizard Magnus. Joining the pair were childhood friends Simon, a blue-skinned mystic; Jimmy, a hulking berserker from the northern mountains; Chuck, the party's thief; and Stu, a ranger, and younger brother of some of Allison's ballet friends.

Somewhere along the way, the group found itself magically transported from the Earth they knew to the fictional game world. After seeing Simon killed in front of them by a brigand's arrow and realizing that they had gained their characters' powers, the friends had no choice but to continue on their quest in the hope that by defeating Magnus they might find their way back home.

While Chuck snoozed in a tree above them, the others were captured by a band of kobolds under the command of Crackrock, an ogre warlord in Magnus' service. After infiltrating the kobold stronghold, the rogue managed to free not only his friends but also a goblin wizard, who proved pivotal to their escape and invited them to his tribe's home to rest and plan.

Not long after the friends resumed their journey east, they rescued a caravan from robbers and agreed to accompany it the rest of the way to Providence City, a local trading hub. Much to their surprise, the five were immediately arrested for aiding wanted criminals and extorted into helping the city's chief of security solve a series of mysterious disappearances.

Only adding to the puzzle was the sudden disappearance of an important relic from the hands of the People, a thousands-strong tribe of former nomads who had recently settled just outside Providence City's walls. Having made fast friends with the son of the People's warlord, the group offered to help them locate their missing artifact.

With the assistance of the warlord's son and a terrified, yet brave, lizardman, the friends solved both mysteries by uncovering and disrupting an underground gladiatorial ring sponsored by a group of the city's elite. While this earned the friends important, powerful, allies and disrupted Magnus' plans to entice Providence City to his side, not all the news was good. The subtle shifts in her friends' personalities that Allison noticed early in their adventure had begun to accelerate. Stu, a ranger, became increasingly uncomfortable within the confines of the city. TJ's vocabulary expanded as he became more aloof from his less erudite companions. At the same time that Jimmy's stature grew into that of a northern berserker, Chuck's shrunk to fit his role as street thief. She herself had changed as well, her powers growing in tandem with her friends'. At least her own memories of the world they'd left behind had not yet begun to fade. So far.

And they were no closer to getting back home.

PROLOGUE

In a forgotten cellar deep beneath the Arcanum's throne room, a rat dragged a discarded sausage back to its nest and the hungry pups within, oblivious to the chaos of the world outside. Several floors above, the servants' children not yet old enough to work played at being grown-up, the boys whacking each other with pretend swords and the girls giving curtseys, each convinced that their futures would be ones of bravery and elegance. Their parents, far more aware of the vagaries of human existence, scurried to and fro among the castle halls, perpetually afraid that they may draw unwanted attention of the master.

And in his throne room, the wizard Magnus sat lazily upon his golden throne, his left leg thrown over an armrest. He sloshed blood-red wine around the goblet in his hand, listening to it slop as he pondered life. At last, his plotting was nearing fruition. The other mages within the Arcanum had been destroyed or sworn oaths of servitude, leaving him the sole authority in the east. His diplomats had secured alliances with all the neighboring kingdoms willing to join him; those who weren't he had "persuaded" to join his cause through the judicious use assassination, invasion, and rains of magical fire. It was quite remarkable how quickly a nation's populace could be encouraged to rise up and overthrow its government when given the right encouragement.

He refocused his eyes upon the servant below him. Having been deep in thought, he wasn't sure just how long she had been waiting, but he didn't think it was more than fifteen or twenty minutes. It was hard to tell sometimes, as all of his servants looked alike. They scurried about to and fro as if their existences held meaning, when in truth their lives could be snuffed out as easily as an ant by a boot. But they amused him, and had their uses, so he tended to tread lightly about them.

The servant who knelt at the bottom of the dais peeked upward through her long, blond bangs. She was dressed as befit her station, in silks and sable, jewelry sparkling on her ears and around her slight neck. Given the speed with which he seemed to go through stewards and other servants, he wondered idly whether they passed the clothes from one to the next or if each set were freshly tailored to the new officeholder's specifications. Not that it mattered one way or the other, of course, as his treasury was full and only getting fuller. War was expensive, yes, but you only need to pay soldiers who lived long enough to collect their due, and Magnus expected great savings before all was said and done.

"Are the preparations in place?" he asked. The woman raised her gaze at his question.

"Yes, Lord," she replied. "The generals sent word that while they could always use more time and training, they serve at your command and are ready to march west."

"More time and training," the wizard chuckled. "They wish to hedge their bets in case their armies do not perform as expected. 'But Lord,' they will say, 'if only we had three months, six months, a year more to train and prepare, we would have been victorious.'" The woman looked up at him impassively, as if she were not really listening to what he had to say, but rather simply waiting for the next command. He sighed, wondering if he should have left some of his rivals alive, if simply for their ability to hold a conversation.

"As you say, Lord," the servant intoned when she realized he had finished his statement.

He sighed a second time and commanded, "Inform them it is time to march. Let us now put an end to the petty squabbles of this world and unite all peoples under one banner. My banner. Those who choose not to join are to be put to the sword. Those who do choose to join, well, I will let the army's commanders figure out what to do with them. I have no interest in dealing with such trivial matters." He waved a dismissal at her with his free hand and watched her scurry toward the audience hall's exit. Just before she reached the door he called out, "Wait, one more thing!" She immediately froze in place, turned and dropped back to her knees.

"Yes, Lord?" Her voice trembled slightly in her fear that he might have just decided to kill her.

"There is a package, with an item of my own devising, just outside my laboratory. Please ensure that it is delivered to General Marston before he marches. It is to be given to one of his most experienced woodsmen, and I have no doubt he will find it useful." The servant remained kneeling until he added, "That is really all. Now go."

She turned and fled so as to be gone before he could call her back a second time.

Even if the armies were not as ready as they could be, what difference did it make? The march west would set other things in motion, force others' hands. He had grown tired of waiting, and wanted, more than anything, to see what happened next.

"Thank you for meeting us on short notice, Cassius," Allison said to their host. "We have been sitting idle for too long, while Magnus continues to consolidate power. We plan to resume our journey east at first light."

"Are you sure you have to leave right now?" Cassius Hallowell, lord protector of Providence City, looked unconvinced. "I'm not so sure that things are as urgent as you believe them to be."

The gray-haired man sat behind a sturdy oaken desk in what was once a large reception area since commandeered as his new office. "Rank hath its privileges," he had gleefully declared upon making the decision to move his possessions from a cramped room well off the beaten path to these much more spacious accommodations. The battle standards and other campaign trophies from his youth looked much less crowded upon the walls, and the broad windows on both of the longer walls kept the room bathed in a comfortable light year-round. His desk was the same, but the other furniture was new, including a suite of chairs and side tables for entertaining visitors. In his old role as castellan most of the visitors to his office weren't the type to be offered seats, as more often than not he was sentencing them to lengthy prison sentences or worse. Of course that had been before Allison and the others, acting on his behalf, had uncovered an underground gladiatorial arena using abductees as combatants. When it turned out that many of the organizers were among the political elite—including the former Lord Protector—Hallowell's promotion was virtually guaranteed. The fact that he had gained the five friends' aid through extortion and threat of execution had been conveniently glossed over.

"I agree," concurred Edmund, Providence City's new castellan, who half sat, half leaned on one corner of Hallowell's desk. His choice to take on the position was made obvious both because his help had been instrumental in breaking up the gladiatorial ring and because he was the son of the current Warlord of the People, the group of nomads who had established a semi-permanent settlement outside Providence City's walls. Thousands strong, all experienced fighters, they were a cause of great anxiety among the city dwellers. Offering the young man the position had not only defused tensions with his clan but also gave the townsfolk an opportunity to get to know their new neighbors. In the short time since Edmund had taken on the castellan's role he had gained the trust of merchants and nobles alike with his quick wit and friendly demeanor. And since he helped lead the assault that rescued Hallowell from imprisonment, he even got to sit on his boss's desk when the doors were closed and only friends were around. He continued, "We have yet to hear back from any of our messengers to the other city states about their intentions for the upcoming war. Unless we can count on their joining us in battle we can't commit much in the way of support for you. There's little sense in marching out to defeat one enemy only to have one of our so-called allies swoop in from behind. Another week or two should be plenty of time for their ruling councils to make their decisions and marshal their troops. Surely you can wait that long?"

Allison looked at each of her friends in turn before responding. Since taking command of the force that rescued both her friends and Lord Hallowell from the sewers, she had become something of the unofficial voice of the group. The others' deferral to her had been a great surprise, since at the outset of their adventures she was the least experienced of the five. She had become used to the idol worship inspired by the enchanted ring upon her finger, as one of its powers was an aura of majesty that inspired awe in common people. Her friends, as well as the two other men in the room, were nowhere close to "common," so should not have been affected by its power. Perhaps her shared backstory with Jimmy helped to create the effect. Her character was an acolyte at the Earth Goddess' temple, and her training there no doubt came with improved poise and strength of personality. Or, she mused, perhaps she had simply proved herself to be someone the boys respected to speak for them. With all the ways they had each changed since coming to this world she couldn't be sure what the reason was.

"No," she asserted. "It's time for us to go. As much as we appreciate your hospitality and your offer of aid, the longer we wait, the longer Magnus has to grow his power and bully others into joining him. We approach the point after which any preparations will be futile—he will simply roll over us with his massive army. We must end this before his forces become insurmountable." Her friends nodded their agreement from where they sat, with the exception of Stu. As of late he had taken up the habit of pacing back and forth, avoiding eye contact with anyone even when speaking directly to them. He moved like a caged tiger, Allison had mused more than once. The way he walked, the way he talked...he was staying with them through sheer force of will alone. Although she didn't say it aloud, her worry that they might lose their friend completely was a significant part of her motivation to leave the city. "Even if the five of us don't travel all the way to the Arcanum, we can at the very least cause mischief that buys you additional time to rally support from your neighbors."

Chuck spoke up for the first time since the meeting had begun. "Mischief ... I like the sound of that." He raised his goblet in a toast and winked. "We all agree with Allison, Cassius. You know our talents, and you know they are being wasted as we sit around waiting for your emissaries to scuttle back and forth. You say another week or two, but you said the same thing two weeks ago."

Jimmy nodded vigorously as his small friend spoke, then added, "Admit it, Eddie. If you or your father were in our position, would you stay behind walls or would you charge forth to meet the enemy head on?" Then, with a mischievous grin, he continued, "Or do you only do that to poor defense-less wizards walking down the street, minding their own businesses?" The reference to the fist fight Edmund and his friends started with TJ when they first met caused the Lord Protector to sputter and choke on the wine in his mouth.

When Hallowell regained his composure, he leaned over to clap his castellan on the back.

"He's got you pegged, Edmund. Maybe you've been among us city folk too long? You getting soft?" The younger man smiled ruefully at the jibe, but didn't take the bait.

"I'd rather say that I've become more strategic in my thinking," he replied, returning Jimmy's smile. "Anyway, if that's your final decision, then I guess it is what it is. Put together a list of equipment that you need, and I'll have the city's quartermaster assemble it for you. Unless you need something outlandish, I should be able to have everything ready tomorrow, or at the latest, the following day."

TJ rose, gave a courtly bow and said, "We thank you for your consideration." He turned and swept out of the room, his robes flapping as he walked. His abrupt departure caught everyone off guard, including Stu, who had appeared completely lost in his own thoughts.

"What was that about, do you think?" he murmured. Then, as if unaware of the irony, gave his own, shallower bow and followed after his friend.

Allison rose to leave, and the other two boys took the cue to finish their drinks. "I know you think this is the wrong decision," she began, her gaze moving back and forth between the two men charged with Providence City's security. "But trust me, we're doing the right thing. Just promise me that if Ik'tha'bor and his tribe turns back up, you'll make sure they're well taken care of. We owe everything to his bravery." She held their gazes in turn until each nodded his assent, then she left the room, Jimmy and Chuck in her wake.

The two leaders sat in silence for several long seconds before

Edmund finally spoke. "That one's got some spark to her, that's for sure."

Hallowell grunted, "Let's just hope it doesn't get snuffed."

Back in their quarters within the palace, the five friends set to organizing and packing their gear. Part of their reward for saving Hallowell from the kidnappers had been to move out of their rooms at the Dancing Unicorn and into a larger, more comfortable suite of rooms in the central castle. Habib, the Dancing Unicorn's innkeeper, argued loudly against their planned move, though they all knew his protests were only for show. The friends had brought nothing but trouble to his inn, and he'd been eager to get back to business as usual.

Their new rooms shared a single common area and a heavily bolted door to the castle halls, providing them greater security as they slept. Guards posted outside their doors should have been sufficient, but a large chunk of the former government was in prison or had been executed, and it wasn't beyond the pale that there could still be members of the Watch in league with the conspirators. The suite's living area was furnished with posh chairs arranged around a large hearth, as well as a full dining suite. Windows looked down upon a well maintained topiary garden, hedge shrubs cut into both geometric shapes and the bodies of varied animals. All in all, these were by far the best accommodations they had stayed in since starting the game.

Arrayed across the dining table were weapons of various sizes and shapes, as well as other tools necessary for their journey. The list included both mundane and magical items ranging from a grappling hook and several hundred feet of light, strong rope to healing potions and magical torches that could burn underwater. Chuck sat by the fireplace, passing his daggers across a whetstone across one last time while Allison and Jimmy quietly discussed what other supplies they might need. TJ had retreated to his room after muttering something about meditating, and Stu had fallen uncharacteristically still. He sat, eyes closed, in one of the chairs across from Chuck, softly humming to himself.

Allison broke the silence. "Do you guys think we can actually do this?" She waved her hand at the equipment scattered across the table.

"What, pack?" Jimmy looked at her in surprise, his response sending Chuck into a tittering fit.

"No, goof," she replied. "All of this." She waved more expansively at the world around them. "Complete the quest. Defeat the wizard. Get back home."

At her mention of home, the boys' faces shifted slightly, as if the reminder that they had once lived different lives shifted the balance in their heads between their old personalities and their new. Allison noticed subtle changes in their postures as well. Her friends suddenly carried themselves less like the men they were and more like boys they had been. She wondered if they saw the same changes in her.

"Of course we can, Allie," Stu replied from his chair by the hearth. "We have to." For a moment all the layers of woodsman were peeled away, leaving only her old friend. "We can't stay here forever." He gazed around the room, and as he did the layers settled back upon him, giving his statement two meanings. The fifteen-year-old was eager to go home, and the woodsman was eager to leave the congested city and return to the nature he loved. If either Chuck or Jimmy noticed the change, neither commented.

"Yeah, you're right, Stu," she said quietly as she turned back to the gear on the table. "We all need to get out of here, don't we?"

CHAPTER 2

The sun shone warmly upon the five friends, though a slight chill in the breeze that raised goosebumps on exposed arms signified the oncoming autumn. The group stood just inside the gates to the city, joined by both Edmund and Hallowell, as well as their personal guards. While it didn't have the pomp of an honor guard sending off victorious heroes, there was a sense of finality in the air. Some passers-by looked on curiously as they walked; while most of the city had heard the basics of what had happened within the sewers, many of the details had been held back for security reasons. Rather than attributing the victory to a group of strangers of uncertain origin, the lord protector's network had circulated rumors that he had let himself be kidnapped from his office as a way of forcing the conspirators to show their hand. He had then led an uprising of the other prisoners, along with help from Edmund and the People. Most of Providence's residents dismissed those rumors as absurd, but five foreigners risking their lives on behalf of people they'd never met was hardly any more likely. It seemed, the friends decided, that there weren't many heroes in this world.

"Every time we start to get comfortable somewhere, it's time to go," Allison murmured to her friends as they double checked the straps on their horses' packs. "It seems like only yesterday we were saying farewell to the Bonecrushers. How many more friends are we going to make only to leave behind as we move on?"

"Oh, chin up, Allie," Chuck replied. "At least we're headed in the right direction. Not much farther and this will all be over, and we can settle down to a nice quiet life."

Beside him, Jimmy guffawed. "Speak for yourself, little man. There is still too much of the world to see for me to settle down quite yet."

TJ nodded. "So much to see and so much knowledge yet to gain. Considering how much I have learned in just the last few months of traveling, I can't imagine what I may yet discover."

"Are you three for real?" Allison stomped her foot. "Settle down? See? Learn? I just want to get back home to my home in the suburbs, my dog, and my parents. If, after that, I never travel farther than to the local grocery store, I'll live and die a happy girl." Her statement had an immediate impact on the others.

"Well, of course that's what I meant," TJ stuttered, his eyes flickering between the other three boys. "I miss my home and family, too. And I can't wait to find our way back." Even Stu, who had been yearning for the outdoors since the moment they set foot in Providence City, turned away from his horse and chimed in.

"Pop Tarts," he said. "I really miss Pop Tarts." He'd never been the most vocal of the five in the first place, so she didn't begrudge him his terseness.

"Let's try to keep that in mind," she replied. From her experiences over just the last few weeks she knew that it wouldn't be long before the characters reasserted themselves and her friends began discussing future plans for the wealth and fame they would get from defeating Magnus once and for all. Even so, she tried to ground them in their real personalities as often as she could. While they were, in fact, the great heroes of the game world, she knew that alone wasn't enough to keep them working toward the end of the quest. Far too many of the computer games she had played with TJ over the years included side quests that took the heroes far afield from what they were *supposed* to be doing: the main plot line.

Hallowell cleared his throat just behind her, startling her from her reverie. She turned as smoothly as possible to hide surprise, though his slight smile suggested he wasn't fooled. "Well, friends," he began, "I regret that I can't send you with more than I have already given. I regret even more than I can't send any of my soldiers with you either. Even the Lord Protector of the city has his limits, and deploying troops to the command of heretofore unknown outsiders is definitely outside said limits." He gave a slight cough. "And even if it weren't, the precarious situation in which we find ourselves, with the Arcanum's forces arrayed against us and no clear commitments from our allies, is a disaster waiting to happen. I hope you all understand."

The five nodded their heads and made agreeing noises, which was about as much as Hallowell expected. After all, they were marching off towards a high likelihood of death, and had long been lobbying for more tangible assistance than well wishes.

Edmund was more tight-lipped than usual, simply nodding and waving at them as they led their horses through the gate. "Funny," Chuck commented. "I kind of expected a bit more enthusiasm from him."

"Yeah," grumbled Jimmy. "After what we did for his people, I expected a fist bump at the very least." Stu let out a snort, and soon they were all chuckling despite themselves. When Edmund had tried to pick a fight with TJ at their first encounter, Jimmy had knocked him unconscious with a single punch to the head. The friends were still chuckling several minutes later as they mounted their horses and set off in earnest.

The group left through the eastern gate, across the city from where they had entered not long before. To the north, the outer edges of the People's encampment was visible, tents flapping lightly in the breeze. The road leading east had only a handful of wagons slowly making their way toward the city, in stark contrast with the long line of travelers and merchant caravans the friends had waited in when they arrived. Trade had clearly dried up with the lands that lay farther east, closer to Magnus' center of power.

"I don't like the looks of this," offered TJ. "Where are the refugees fleeing invading armies? Where are the injured soldiers retreating from battle? If there is fighting to the east, we should see both. If there isn't fighting to the east, where have all the merchants gone? Providence City has always been a trading hub for the entire continent. It's almost as if Magnus somehow cut off all travel westward."

"Or," murmured Chuck, "there's no one left to flee. Perhaps those who fought were all killed or enslaved, and those who didn't fight have been absorbed into his army and kingdom." Allison shivered at the prospect of entire nations subject to such conditions.

"Well this is just one more reason for us to finish our task. In case we needed it." Her statement hung over the friends like a pallor, each lost in their own thoughts about why they were headed into the proverbial lion's den.

As the miles passed beneath them the fertile pastureland on Providence City's outskirts soon gave way to low brush and finally a light woodland. Houses became less frequent until the friends found themselves traveling alone, hemmed in on both sides by trees. Even so, there was still evidence of civilization in the form of the road upon which they rode and tree stumps left by woodcutters. If they hadn't been heading toward potential disaster it would have been an idyllic day. As they rode, the group unconsciously returned to their standard marching order, with Stu in the front and Jimmy in the back, bookending the less skilled combatants from ambush. The sun crept overhead and toward the horizon behind them, lengthening shadows and casting the woods on either side into darkness.

Without warning, Stu pulled his horse up short and raised his hand to signal the others to stop. He cocked his ear to the side, straining to tell if the noise he'd heard was something ominous or just the normal sounds of the woods. As he listened, he calmly unstrapped his bow from its bindings and drew an arrow. To the rear, Jimmy drew his sword and prepared to dismount—their horses were simple riding animals not trained for combat and would be impossible to control in a fight. Of course, even if he rode a war horse, twirling a six-foot-long blade from the back of one's mount just isn't the sort of thing one does. Allison, Chuck, and TJ looked around anxiously, preparing their own fight-or-flight reactions. The five remained still for several tense minutes before Stu shook his head and turned to the others.

"False alarm. I thought I sensed something in the woods alongside us, but I guess not." He grimaced. "Sorry about that, must be nerves." The others relaxed in turn, and they coaxed their horses forward once more. Allison shot a glance toward Chuck and caught him looking at her, an eyebrow raised. She eased her horse closer to her friend to share a quiet word.

"Nerves?" She asked doubtfully.

"I don't believe that for a minute," Chuck replied. "He's been strung tighter than his bow for the last month, nearly begging to get out of the city. This is the most relaxed I've seen him in a long time. Maybe he's second guessing himself, but I'd put money on his instincts." The small man made a show of stretching his neck, glancing casually into the trees to either side before returning his attention to Allison. "I don't think it's a great idea to let down our guard quite yet."

Allison nodded her agreement, and as she guided her horse away from Chuck's she made a point of placing a hand on her mace.

The road continued on at a slight incline, and when Stu reached the top of the rise he once again reined in his horse and took his bow in hand. The others trotted forward to discover the cause of his concern: about a hundred yard farther along the road a group of men and women, armed to the teeth, were arrayed across the road. Most looked west toward where the five had paused. A pair of draft horses stood in front of a wagon, and a line of steeds tethered to a makeshift picket cropped grass contentedly. "Dammit," Stu muttered. "I knew something was wrong back there. It must have been one of their scouts."

"Maybe they're just here to shake down travelers for whatever gold they're carrying." Allison asked hopefully. "Maybe they'll let us pass instead of fighting. Sure, they outnumber us, but they won't all live through a battle if it comes to it."

Beside her Chuck shook his head. "No, I don't see it playing out that way. If Stu really heard one of their scouts, they've been waiting for us. The fact that they haven't already moved off the road to let us pass means they're not gonna." He squinted to get a better look at them, then continued, "I see about twenty. No bows, but there's no guarantee they don't have a few hidden in that wagon."

TJ snorted and nudged his horse forward towards the waiting group. "If they're going to sit there all bunched up like that, I'll clear 'em right out." He turned and winked at the others, a boyish grin creeping across his face. "Looks like classic fireball formation to me. Just need to move a little bit closer to get in range."

"Sounds to me like you've got the right idea," Jimmy laughed, kicking his horse into a trot to catch up. Stu continued to peer at the group in the road below, scowling slightly, but joined the others in following TJ. Their approach didn't appear to cause the other group alarm; rather, they continued to stand at their ease, some leaning against the wagon and several relaxing in the grass to the side. Two were deep in conversation, and a third nearby burst into laughter at something one of them said.

TJ had crossed about half the distance before pulling his horse up short. He squinted, eying the distance to confirm that he was close enough for his magic to reach the other group. His hand reached to the reagents pouch on his belt to draw the material components that helped channel his more powerful incantations. As he began a series of chants and complex hand gestures, one of the people by the wagon turn to wave at them. Sudden realization dawned on Allison and with a yell she threw herself off her horse toward TJ. Her armor-clad body knocked him sideways from his saddle and to the ground, his disrupted spell exploding outward. The blast threw Allison to the side, toppled both their confused horses, and thoroughly scorched TJ's robes. The pair lay stunned for several long seconds while the others looked on in surprise.

"What did you do that for?" TJ yelled when he managed to regain his equilibrium. His eyes glowed red as he glared at Allison, and a bright nimbus of power blossomed on his hands as if he were going to attack her next. She cried out and threw her hands in front of her face protectively. The fear on her face made TJ lower his own hands and his countenance returned to normal, the light disappearing from his fingers. A look of horror passed over him at what he had almost done.

"Allie," he began, "I'm sorry." Slowly, Allison lowered her guard and took a deep breath. She gave him a half-hearted smile and slowly staggered to her feet.

Three of the people from the group below ran towards them, spurring Chuck to slide off his horse for cover. Stu tentatively raised his bow, though his attention was focused more on TJ and Allison than on the approaching danger. "It's okay, TJ. You just reacted. That's how you stay alive in a place like this." Allison continued, then took another breath. "I didn't think I had the time to keep you from attacking them any other way. Look." She pointed at the approaching figures. "That's Tilly. She was one of Edmund's fighters with me in the sewers when we rescued you, and without her we never would have made it out."

Stu, with his ranger's eyes, came to the same conclusion and lowered his bow. By the time the trio had arrived, weapons had been stowed and the tension in the air was replaced by smiles and handclasps.

"What just happened?" Tilly asked breathlessly. The petite raven-haired woman was clad in the combination of chain and leather that had become popular with the younger members of the People. Her sword remained sheathed, but she kept her hand close to the hilt as if she were looking for a reason to draw steel. "We saw the explosion but there's no one attacking."

"Just a little misunderstanding," Allison replied cheerfully. Now that the crisis had passed, her smile for TJ was considerably more genuine. "We got it all sorted out, though. It's all better now."

One of the others with Tilly, a tall brown-haired man also in leather and chain, looked sidelong his leader. "Are you sure this was a good idea?" He nodded toward TJ and added, "Those magic types aren't to be trusted in the best of times. This one looks like he's gone a little crazy." His hand rested conspicuously on his sword's hilt. The third, a similarly clad woman, rolled her eyes and shrugged, as if to say that those sorts of questions were either beneath her dignity or above her pay grade.

"Stand down, Cailin," Tilly replied. "They're good. Lady Allison and I go way back, and her friends are good with me." She slapped Allison on the shoulder. "Ain't that right?" Her voice was relaxed, but surreptitiously raised an eyebrow at the healer to confirm that things really were okay.

"Yeah, it's all good. Like I said, a bit of a misunderstanding." She grinned wickedly. "TJ was about to incinerate you all, and I stopped him just in time."

The young man's eyes widened. "Um, that's not making me feel any better, you know." He let out a slight chuckle, but it was obviously forced.

Jimmy stepped forward and said with a laugh, "You get used to it, really. We've been traveling together for years and he hasn't killed me yet." The big man nodded in agreement with himself, then tugged on his horse's reins and began down the hill to where the rest of Tilly's group waited anxiously. The others followed suit, with the exception of TJ, whose horse wanted nothing more to do with him. Rather, it trotted along the side of the road while he stomped sullenly along on foot.

CHAPTER 3

The sun had dipped low enough on the horizon that the group decided to camp for the evening rather than push on any further. They left the wagon in the middle of the road—there was little chance that anyone would be traveling this way during the night—and built a cheery fire just off the beaten path. A clear sky promised a dry night, and spirits were high as they sat around the blaze renewing friendships. Tilly ordered a cask of ale tapped, which added considerably to everyone's mood. At last Allison raised the question that had been on all her friends' minds.

"So, um, I don't mean to suggest that we're not happy to see you, but what are you doing here? Does the warlord know that you left the encampment? You realize that we have got a long, long road ahead of us, don't you?"

"Edmund told me that you were leaving, but that his father hadn't made any decisions about what the People will do." Tilly took a deep drink from her ale and let out a contented sigh. "That's the spot." She smacked her lips. "But everyone knows that when all is said and done, honor dictates that we follow you into battle. After what you did for us, there isn't any other option." At this, the others from the tent city nodded or raised mugs in toasts to the five friends. "But just because we know that's how it's going to turn out doesn't mean it will happen on our own schedule. I imagine the warlord is waiting for the same confirmation that the city folks are: that if our fighters march to war, those we leave behind won't be killed, or worse. There's a difference between following one's honor and being a fool. Neither of those men are fools.

"So, I and a few of my friends decided to go on an extended patrol, if you will. We're scouting out east to search for potential danger to our people. After all, the best decisions are made with the best information," she finished. "And that's why we're here."

"Well, on behalf of all five of us, please believe me when I say that we are grateful," Allison began, "but, when the warlord learns that you have marched off without permission, isn't he going to be angry?" Her question sent the others into a fit of laughter and back slapping that went on for some time. When they finally settled down, Allison looked at Tilly quizzically, still waiting for an answer.

"Oh lady," replied a large brutish man whose every inch of exposed skin was covered in scars. "The warlord may be in charge, but he doesn't own us. Any of us are free to come or go as they wish, so long as they aren't expected to be somewhere in particular." He also took a moment to take a swig from his cup. "Of course, even if we weren't allowed to leave, it's not going to be a problem for us."

"Why's that?" Asked Chuck.

"'Cause chances are we'll all be dead long before we make it back to our home anyway. It's not like he can kill us twice!" The man let out a guffaw and raised his cup. Several others, including Jimmy, let out a cheer and smacked their own cups against his, sending foam and ale in all directions.

"Ahh," Chuck replied, less than satisfied with the answer.

"Oh, things can't be that bad, can they?" Allison asked. She looked to her friends for support. "We're the heroes, aren't we? That ought to give us a fighting chance. What's the fun if there's no chance of winning?" As usual, references to the world back home yielded confused looks from the locals, but this time Allison was certain she saw slight waves of confusion dance across her friend's faces as well.

"Well I don't know about heroes," Jimmy replied, "but I haven't been killed yet, and Magnus isn't the first wizard I've gone toe-to-toe against. Assuming we can get close enough to him, I imagine he can get chopped in half just as easily as anyone else."

"That's the trick, isn't it?" Stu broke his silence. "There's several hundred miles to travel, through increasingly hostile territory. The roads may be clear now, but it's only a matter of time before we start running into armed bands marching west or wreaking havoc around the countryside. We have to find out where he is, travel there, and get past his guards. Only then will you get that chance to chop him up."

"Not to mention magical wards," TJ chimed in.

Stu nodded at his friend. "Not to mention magical wards."

"So what are you all saying?" Allison cried out. "We just give up the quest and let Magnus take over the world? If he's even half as crazy as we've heard, what sort of world would that be?" The others stared back at her, and she was surprised to discover that she was standing up, one of her fists raised. Several of the People gazed at her in awe, but even those unswayed by her ring's power took her seriously. Most nodded in agreement.

"Don't get me wrong, Lady," the scarred man replied. He put down his mug and extended his hands, palms forward, in a placating gesture. "I never meant to say that I didn't think we should go and fight for all we're worth. I don't want my own children living in a world run by that wizard." He looked cautiously at TJ before continuing, "or any wizard, for that matter. But I've been known to take odds from time to time, and if I were casting the bones on this, I wouldn't take the wager that we live to see it through."

"And that," continued Tilly, "is what sets us apart from those city folk. I'm not afraid to die. Thom there is not afraid to die. None of us are. If we were, we wouldn't have come." The others nodded grimly. "What I'm afraid of is living out a long life and lying on my death bed knowing that not was my debt to you unfulfilled, but that I could have satisfied that debt and at the same time make things better for my clan. When I cross to the other side, I want the gods to be proud of what I did, and I want to be proud of it too."

The five friends sat silently, each digesting the young fighter's declaration. Her words were unsurprising to both Stu and Jimmy, and they nodded knowingly. Both had grown up with similar codes, Jimmy to his own clan in the north and Stu to his adoptive parents and the village they protected as the king's foresters. Chuck, in contrast, fought to suppress a smirk. His own code revolved around self-preservation above all else, having cared about only one other person in his entire career before meeting Jimmy and TJ at a tavern. For his part, TJ was lost in thought, as if he had spent the last several minutes thinking over some minutiae of arcane theory and hadn't heard a word of what had passed. To Allison, however, the idea that someone would choose to throw their life away for her sake was almost too much.

"Well, thank you," she sniffled, as her nose had suddenly gone runny. "We are grateful for your company."

"Hear, hear!" Thom called out. Another clatter of mugs followed.

The reunion went deep into the night, and featured many more such clatters.

CHAPTER 4

Early the next morning the group woke to aching heads but uplifted hearts. What had seemed like an unlikely, almost insurmountable challenge had become a bit more realistic. Thom's declaration that they were all likely to die did, in fact, take a little shine off the silver lining, but their chances had clearly improved, and that made a big difference.

Tillie had brought twenty volunteer fighters with her, all battle tested. Some, like Thom, showed open evidence of their prior combat experience through scars or burns, whereas others' experience was visible in the tense, alert way they carried themselves as they went about their daily activities. These men and women had killed and seen friends killed in turn and were ready for anything. About a quarter of them had participated in the sewer raid. These paid special deference to Allison, having seen her take the lead in spite of the injuries she had received beforehand.

"It must be exhausting to always be on edge like that,"

Allison murmured to Stu as they watched several of their new companions finish breaking camp.

Her friend gave a single nod and replied, "But not as bad as being dead." He left her side to attend to his horse, and as he walked away Allison noticed for the first time that Stu moved in a manner very similar to the ones she had pointed out. She shuddered involuntarily at unbidden thoughts about what her friend's past must have been like. Perhaps he would share that story with them as they traveled. With hundreds of miles to go, they were going to spend many nights around a similar fire, and the ale would eventually run out. All they would have for entertainment would be their own company.

The sun was still low in the eastern sky when the group resumed their trek east. They had no specific plan as to where they were going or what they would do when they got there, but given the distance they needed to travel, there would be plenty of time to determine specifics as they went.

"Thom is my second," Tilly shared as they rode. The tattooed man turned in his saddle and gave a little wave at the sound of his name.

"Your second?" TJ asked, surprise in his voice. He looked back and forth between the two figures: one slight and wiry, the other bulky and battle hardened. Jimmy cringed at his question and guided his horse a few lengths away in case Tilly decided to explode. He'd often been bested by a particular girl when he was a boy, and she had continued to beat him when they were young adults.

Tilly, however, took it without insult, and in fact seemed amused by his assumption. "Thom has attempted on more than one occasion to take my position by way of challenge, though not lately. Many of those scars he so proudly bears are my own handiwork." Her mouth split into a grin. "So yes, he is my second."

"Ahh." Was the best response TJ could muster.

"Pshaw, there's no hard feelings. Thom and I trained together and have fought together for years. Believe it or not, although he looks like he's been dragged behind a horse for a few miles we've seen the same number of winters. I'd trust my life to any of the ones here with us, but I'd give my life for his."

Tilly paused a moment to let TJ reply, and when his mouth stayed closed she said, "Not everyone from my company joined us, as they had other obligations. Several have young children, and at least two are pregnant. On the other hand, about a half dozen follow other captains, but joined me when they learned of our plans." She pointed at a threesome up ahead who chatted as they rode. "Those up there were among the spearmen who stood with Lady Allison and me at the battle in the sewers, though I imagine you didn't notice them, being prisoners and all. Afner, on the left, was hit in his shoulder by an arrow, and Inga, in the middle, nearly died from blood loss after taking a sword in her groin. She credits you, Allison, for saving her life. She is shy, though, and is somewhat awed by your presence, so she keeps her distance." Now that Allison thought about it, she had noticed the pretty fighter glancing their way every so often but had assumed the gaze was for Tilly. She made a mental note to speak with the woman when they made camp. The last thing any of them needed was a star-struck moonchild when things got hairy. A quest was no place for hero worship, pun intended.

"Wait," Allison interrupted. "Did you actually announce that you were leaving? You didn't even sneak out?"

Tilly laughed. "We've been over this, Lady. There is no dishonor in joining you on your journey, and therefore there was no shame in sharing. Short of killing us, neither Edmund nor his father could have stopped us, and that presumes that they would want to. In truth, were it not for their own obligations to the People and to the city, they'd probably be here as well.

"Angus," she pointed to the brown-cloaked man riding several hundred yards ahead of the group, "is an excellent scout. He has a way of sniffing out danger that's almost witchcraft—though don't tell him I said that. I've never seen anyone better, to be honest." Stu gave a little snort, to which she replied, laughing, "He's the one you *didn't* see following you along the road yesterday. Angus didn't leave your side once from the moment you passed through the city gates. Now that would've been a lucky break for him if your wizard friend had succeeded in killing us all with fire."

"Honest mistake," TJ said distractedly, then fell silent again.

"Yeah," she sounded unconvinced. "So you said. You already met Cailin and his sister Cait. They were the pair that came with me after the, erm, honest mistake." She looked sidelong at TJ. "You may have guessed that he's the more cautious of the two, but they're both seasoned fighters and reliable allies." Now that Tilly had pointed it out, the resemblance between the two was clear: despite a significant difference in height, they shared both a nose and cheekbones. Their faces were young, so it was difficult to tell which was the older, though how they reacted to TJ's magic suggested that of the two, Cait was the more level-headed.

Tilly listed off the names of the others that had join with her, as well as their specialties. Most were skirmishers, and a few were scouts and trackers. Most noticeably was the man Roland, who rode with a bow across his back.

"I thought your people looked down on archery as beneath their honor," Stu sneered. His hand went to the shaft of the magical bow Chuck had given him.

Times change," Tilly replied, not taking the bait. "There's no denying archery's value, especially when your enemy has bows of their own. When we lived a more nomadic life most of our foes were monstrous humanoids who fought with claw and club. But when you make to charge across hundreds of yards in the open and the other side is raining arrows upon you, your worldview changes. It seems that our clan should now be worried less about orcs and more about armies."

"There was a company of archers in the sewers as well," Allison reminded him.

Stu nodded, a slight smile creeping across his face in vindication.

"I can't help but notice," chimed in Chuck, "that none of your paint-and-feather wearing folks came along. By my math that means Allison is our only healer. Not that I'm complaining or anything, cause she's pretty great actually, but it seems like there may be a bit of a flaw in this plan. I don't think she's going to be able to keep all of us up and going if things get hairy." He glanced at Allison, as if to say that she better prior-itize her friends over the new folks. She rolled her eyes at him in return.

Tilly sighed in frustration. "Yes, this is less than ideal. Our mystics do not always share our perspective on the duties of honor. When I asked for volunteers from their ranks I received only silence." She shook her head. "So, you're correct. We'll have to rely on Lady Allison alone for any magical healing we need. But don't forget that we—every one of us—is battle-tested. Most of us know how to set a bone, and we all know how to bind up a wound. Angus is talented at herblore, as I imagine, is your friend Stu. We will make do with what we have."

"Does that seem a little ungrateful to you?" Chuck pressed. "After all, it was their mystical artifact that we retrieved. I'd have expected them, out of any of you, to be the ones lining up to help us."

"You would think, wouldn't you?" she replied. "And here's where their sense of honor diverges. If anything, they feel slighted that such an important item could be lost from their ownership only to be recovered by outsiders. Word is that you didn't make the best impression on them when you first got involved. I heard something about a pompous wizard or something."

"That sounds about right to me," quipped Chuck. He paused to stroke his chin, "Though, to be fair, it could really be referring to any wizard." TJ shook his head and snorted.

"So, long story short, they decided not to aid us. If and when the Warlord decides to march east, they will, of course, come along. But I think more than one of them would be just as happy to let you all die in the meanwhile."

"Well, I will do my best," Allison said. "I feel like I've done a pretty good job so far, at least. I'll try not to let you down."

"We have every faith in you, Lady Allison."

"As do we, Lady Allison," Chuck mimicked with a giggle, then trotted his horse forward, ignoring the both women's scowls at his mockery.

CHAPTER 5

When the sun touched the western horizon, the group again made camp just off the road. They'd seen no others the entire day, and there was little sign that the road had been used recently, so everyone agreed that moving to the cover of the woods was more effort than necessary. This gave Stu and a few of the others the opportunity to hunt for fresh meat for the stew burbling in a pot over their smile fire. The wagon was well stocked with supplies such as potatoes and dried meat, but they didn't know how scarce food might get as they traveled further east and wanted to ration themselves. Besides, no one actually enjoyed trail food, so any excuse to eat fresh game was always well received.

After everyone had had their fill and mugs were filled with ale (also well stocked in the wagon), Jimmy and Chuck shared with the others the story of how the five of them had ended up at Providence City in the first place, with Allison and Tilly picking up the story at the point where the attack in the sewers began. From time to time, Afner or Inga would chime in with a piece of information, the latter being especially grateful for Allison having saved her life. When the story was done, the group settled into a companionable silence, only disturbed by a belch or two and the sound of several of the People sucking on pipe stems.

"So," Thom broke the silence tentatively, equal parts curiosity and anxiety in his voice. "What's the plan?" He looked around the campfire at each of the friends in turn and the anxiety took over completely. "There *is* a plan, isn't there? We could easily have pushed on another hour or so before we lost the light, which means we're in no great hurry to get anywhere in particular."

Several of the others around the fire looked mildly scandalized at his question, particularly the younger ones more likely to be affected by Allison's enchanted ring. Tilly nodded and added, "That is a good question. What are your thoughts about how to move forward?" Her voice was less incredulous than was her second's, clearly giving them the benefit of the doubt.

The question hung awkwardly in the air for several long seconds as the five looked back and forth between each other. At last Jimmy spoke up. "Well the obvious solution would be to kill Magnus." His declaration was met by stoic faces, and Thom visibly rolled his eyes. Jimmy pressed on, "The trick is of course how to get close enough do it, and once we're there, how do we actually pull it off?" He paused, hoping someone else would take up the thread.

"Any number of ways, really," offered Chuck. "As the great philosopher Steven Brust once said, 'No matter how subtle the wizard, a knife between the shoulder blades will seriously cramp his style.' So I guess that's one option."

"That's not my question," pressed Thom. "Of course we can stab him, shoot him, explode him into goo," he pointed at Chuck, Stu, and TJ in turn. "But do you even know where he is? How to get to him? How he's guarded? You can't do any of that until you've answered all those questions."

"Yeah, well," Allison began, her mind racing for a clever response but coming up empty. "The truth is that we don't know. We've got hundreds of miles to cover before we even get close, and it won't be long before we get into territory under his sway. At that point we'll be fighting through or sneaking past all manner of things, if our experiences with Magnus' minions so far are any indication. You're right that we don't even know where he is, and we're going to have to figure it out at some point along the way. But if I'm being honest right now, preparing for a final showdown with him isn't exactly the furthest thing in mind, but it's definitely a pretty distant ninth or tenth."

Tilly leaned forward. "So let me get this straight. Your plan for defeating the mad wizard hell bent on conquering the world is to just march east until you run into him, and then you'll figure something out?"

Allison's face grew red and she clenched her fists. "Yes, that's exactly what we're going to do. It's worked pretty well so far. We started marching east, not really looking for trouble and the next thing we knew we had killed one of Magnus' lieu-tenants and scattered a tribe of kobolds. Then, we started marching east again and what happened? We indirectly over-threw a government considering allying itself with him and at the same time saved your collective bacon by returning your knickknack on a stick." At this she stood up, pointing at Thom and Tilly in turn. "And you know what? We were going to do that before you folks showed up, and now that you're here we're *still* going to do that, because this is *our* quest and no one ever invited you in the first place. Hell, you were just talking about how this is a suicide mission anyway. If you aren't happy with our plan, then you can just take off because I'm not going to take any crap from any of you." Her chest heaved from shouting and her face had turned a bright red. An uneasy quiet reigned around the fire, even the crickets having been stunned into silence.

Thom slowly began to clap. Then Tilly joined in, and soon all of the members of the clan were applauding wholeheartedly and whooping with delight. When the noise had settled down, Thom said to his commander with a wide grin, "You were right. This one knows how to take command, and we could do far worse than to follow her."

Allison, unsure of what had just happened, returned to her seat and took a deep drink of water. Stu patted her on her back.

"Well, okay then. I guess that's settled," she concluded with a curt nod.

CHAPTER 6

Over the following days the group settled into a routine. Each morning they would break camp with the rising sun, spend the day following the road east, and then make camp just before sunset. Stu estimated that they were making fifteen or so miles per day, and while they could have moved faster if they left the wagon behind no one suggested doing so. It was unspoken, but understood, that this was because none of the horses could carry a cask of ale, whereas the wagon could carry many.

The first refugees began to trickle westward along the road nearly a week into their journey. At first there were ones and twos bringing with them no more than their horses could carry, but soon carts hauling families along with all their worldly possessions came bumping along the cobbles. These invariably left the road to go around the friends. Looks of desperation and defeat on the wagon drivers' faces, along with the bandages they wore and the crutches at their sides, made it clear that they had seen all they wanted of armed soldiers. As each cart approached the group the driver nudged its horse or horses to the side and they passed without a single glance, as if they believed that if they didn't make eye contact they would be left alone to get on with their miserable lives.

After an hour or so, during which the stream of migrants only increased, Allison tried to flag one down for information. "Excuse me. Sir?" and "Ma'am, can you help us?" The first half dozen refused to look at her; her enchanted ring couldn't overcome their hesitance to engage in conversation. Finally, she dismounted, stepped off the road, and stood directly in the way of a stooped man leading a one-horse cart stacked high with an assortment of sacks, furniture, and children. The man looked as if he would roll his cart right over the top of her, but Jimmy cleared his throat menacingly and placed a hand on the dagger at his waist. With a deep sigh the bedraggled man stopped and looked at her expectantly.

Allison looked him up and down before speaking, noting that his clothes looked like they had once been of high quality, well-tailored if not actually made from finer cloth. His shoes, while scuffed, had been recently cobbled and when he raised his hands in supplication she noticed that his palms were uncalloused. The laughter wrinkles around his eyes told of a long life happily lived, and the slump in his shoulders and his blank gaze were newly acquired. He stood patiently, but silently, waiting for her to reveal her intentions, much like a recently broken horse. He was a man who had fallen hard and was on the verge of giving up.

"Good sir," she began. "From where are you coming? What is the meaning of all this?" She gestured to the other refugees, who had continued moving forward in their line, which had bent a little further from the road to avoid the temporary blockage. These others neither offered a single word in protest, nor spared the singled-out man a glance, accepting it as just another obstacle. "And what news can you tell us of the east?"

The man squinted and gave a halfhearted laugh that might once have been mocking, but now just seemed resigned. "This road only goes one direction, and we're headed west, so we must be coming from the east, wouldn't you say?" Maybe the ring was having an effect, because he seemed to regret his words almost immediately and gave a little head bob in apology before continuing, "From Reynoldstown, M'Lady. The armies came from further east. Company after company marched toward us until we could barely see the earth from the number of bodies camped outside our walls. We hoped they would just make us bend the knee and then move on." He shrugged. "Which king or warlord or crazy wizard rules us rarely makes a difference in the daily lives of the common folk, so those of us on the Council opened the gates and let them in. There were so many of them, they were going to capture us anyway. Why subject ourselves to misery and death in the meanwhile, you understand?" His eyes bored into her, begging her to agree that they had made the right decision. She nodded her head and placed a hand on his shoulder.

"Of course," she replied. "You did what you thought best for your people. I would have done the same, as there is no honor in dooming those you are sworn to protect for the sake of fighting a lost cause."

He seemed to take comfort in her words, the sorrow and pain on his face lifting ever so slightly. "We were fools." He turned and spat, the regret and defeat washing back over him. "As soon as the first soldiers marched through the gate, they began to press our young men into service and march them out to become part of the assault on the next city. When all those who could put up a fight had been taken away and only the weakest among us remained, the slaughter began. The elderly, women, children ... anyone they didn't think useful was killed where they stood." Tears fell from his eyes, leaving trails on his dusty cheeks. "What good is an artist, or even a tailor or cobbler or weaver, if they are too old to march with the army? They're nothing more than extra mouths to feed when rations are already tight."

"How did you and all these others escape?"

He laughed at the question. "Why would they try to stop us? Anywhere that takes us in will just have to feed us. Now we are someone else's problem to deal with."

Chuck commented from his saddle, "Huh. You'd think they'd want what they do to the cities they capture to remain secret. If it were me, I would want the next city to open their gates up just the way you did. And the next one after that." Allison frowned at him, and he followed with, "I didn't say I would actually do it, just that it doesn't make sense. Sheesh."

The man laughed bitterly. "He is not wrong, Lady. I have asked myself the same thing this whole time. They know word will spread. You know what I think? I think they don't care. I think they're just as happy to climb the walls and fight as they are to be invited in. After all, it will be our ... my children who will die in the assault. That's the kind of insanity that wizard brings." He looked skyward for a moment then shook his head. "If I still believed in the gods I would say this Magnus trying to bring about the end of the world. But after what I've seen, I have time for neither gods nor prophecies." His eyes bored directly into Allison's. "If you ask me, maybe the end of the world is what's called for. That might just be what is best for all of us right about now." He doffed his cap. "Now, if you would excuse me, Lady, I really must keep moving. Every mouth in front of me in line is one mouth to be fed before mine." He gave her the slightest bow before slapping the reins of his wagon's horse and moving forward. Allison stepped aside to let the vehicle pass. With the blockage removed, the line of refugees returned to its original flow of sad bodies, paying no heed to the armed party headed east.

CHAPTER 7

Sometime overnight the stream of refugees abated, and the friends once again found themselves traveling an empty road. While the land did not yet show active signs of war, the passage of so many desperate people had taken its toll. Most of the low-hanging foliage within a hundred yards of the road had been scavenged for firewood, and anything edible, including roots and even bark, had been foraged. The few homesteads visible from the road had also been ransacked—Stu and Angus explored the first several and reported that anything valuable had been taken, and even the furniture and cabinets had been broken up for fuel. It was as if a swarm of locusts had come through, consuming everything in its path.

Near the end of the day the group came upon another similarly treated farmhouse. Clouds had rolled in, accompanied by a damp chill that promised a miserable, wet night, so rather than pushing forward for another few miles they decided to take shelter from the oncoming rain. The house had four rooms, including a kitchen and two separate bedchambers. Its nearby barn, while also stripped of anything of value, was sturdy and would keep the horses out of the rain. Once the animals had been fed and rubbed down those not assigned to sentry duty retired to the farmhouse, where they spread out bedrolls on all available space. The four rooms shared a central hearth for heat, though the absence of anything to burn rendered it nothing more than a pretty centerpiece. Though simple in design, the building was well constructed from solid materials and it was clear that whoever had lived there had once been successful farmers, merchants, or perhaps both.

"This is so sad," offered Jimmy, as he looked around the room. "So much effort and love went into building this, and all of that is gone. Assuming that whoever lived here still lives at all, they'll find nothing left when they return. What a waste."

Thom grunted. "This is why we like our tents. Anything that you can't pack up and move at a moment's notice can be lost forever. The city folk think themselves better than us, but where are they now? Destitute and homeless, whereas we have our tents and treasures. Who's laughing now, I wonder?" He grinned a toothy grin.

"I don't think any of this is a laughing matter," Allison protested. "Like you said, these people have lost everything. If you ask me, we should feel compassion for them, or at the very least pity." She looked around for support only to discover that TJ had his nose stuck in a book, Stu was nowhere to be found. Chuck sat, cross legged, eyes wide open and staring at nothing in particular.

"Right, guys?" Jimmy asked. When no one responded, he

smacked Chuck across the chest. "Hello? You with us little man?

The smaller man blinked twice and apologized, "Sorry, was just doing a little mind thing someone once taught me. What were you saying?" A glint in his eye suggested he found something funny, but he fell quiet rather than sharing.

Jimmy shook his head, then nodded at Allison in encouragement, and she smiled at him in gratitude.

"You'll have to excuse Thom," Tilly said. "He's among the ones who think that we've already spent too much time in one place. If he had his way, we'd have different leaders who'd be making different decisions. I bet that's why he's with us right now. He got sick of sitting in one place, and by coming with us he gets to ride that angry nag of his instead. Ain't that right, Thom?" This yielded a spate of laughter from the others, though her second waved it away with a grunt.

"We're all entitled to our opinions, aren't we, Captain? Just because my preference lost the challenge and yours won doesn't mean that I am going to change my mind all of a sudden. It just means that I've got to accept what is clearly a stupid decision." He winked with the last sentence and Tilly stuck her tongue out in response.

Both Cait and her brother chuckled at the exchange, and at Allison's concerned look the young woman added, "Don't worry, Lady. They go on like this all the time. They're like an old married couple sometimes."

"She wishes!" retorted Thom, and the entire room burst into laughter.

TJ looked up from his reading and said, "Well at least we can all appreciate the fact that we have a roof over our heads instead of being out in tents in the rain." This elicited a bevy of agreeing noises from the others in the room. Then a companionable silence descended on the group, each lost in their own thoughts. Thunder cracked outside, rattling the walls and the sound of a sudden downpour beat against the roof.

The door burst open and a small figure staggered in, followed by Stu. Both were drenched to the bone, and whereas the dampness didn't appear to bother Stu at all, the person he had brought in looked like nothing so much as a wet cat, dejected and miserable. Stu gave the newcomer a slight shove, and in the light of the room's lamps the figure was revealed to be a waif-like girl. At first glance she looked to be no more than ten, but slight swells to her chest suggested that she was perhaps a little bit older. Her blond, shoulder length hair was plastered to her face and neck, her clothes scuffed and torn, and Allison's healer instincts drew her eyes downward to the girl's unshod feet to discover that that several of her toenails had recently fallen out. Black blood beneath others suggested that the remaining nails were soon to follow.

"Found her sneaking around the barn," Stu offered. He glanced around the room once before nodding and slipping silently back outside. The girl looked like she wanted to follow him, as she gazed at the hardened faces of the men and women surrounding her. With a sigh of despair she let her knees crumple beneath her and dropped to the ground.

Silence reigned, no one knowing quite how to react to the sudden appearance of the girl. The group had gotten used to keeping to their own company and looked at each other in confusion. Allison's eyes met Tilly's, who gave the younger woman a nod. Allison stood and slowly crossed the floor to where the girl sat slumped. She knelt down next to the still figure, and said softly, "Hello little one. My name is Allison." The girl remained quiet and after several seconds Allison laid a hand lightly on her shoulder. When this, too, yielded no reaction, she and took the girl's chin in her fingers and turned her face upwards. Green eyes stared blankly back at her, echoing the defeat in the child's posture.

"I'm Allison," she repeated. "What's your name, sweetie? Are you hungry, or maybe thirsty?" Allison slid her hand up from the girl's chin to brush away the wet hair splayed across her cheek. With a slight quirk of a smile she amended, "Well, perhaps not thirsty." Thom approached the pair and lay a small wallet of dried meat on the ground, then backed away as if afraid of spooking a wild animal. Allison gave him a quick nod in gratitude, and withdrew a piece of jerky. "Here, take this," she said, pressing the food into the girl's hand. Quick as a flash, the morsel went into her mouth, and her jaw chewed methodically. Once she had swallowed the food Allison handed her a second piece.

Chuck, who had woken from his nap when the door flew open, slipped outside. Not long later, he returned with an armful small wooden boards. "The boys out there helped me tear these off the barn's walls. Figured no one'll miss them any time soon." In short order, he had a small fire crackling in the hearth, and when Allison gave the girl's hand a little tug, she willingly resettled near the blaze. There, her clothes immediately began to give off steam as they dried.

Several long minutes of awkward silence passed while the

girl silently sat shivering by the fire. Just as Allison made to stand, the girl offered, "Becka."

"Hmm?" Allison asked, squatting back down.

"That's my name. Becka." The girl leaned her head against Allison's shoulder and let out a small sigh.

Allison gave the girl a few seconds to offer more information, then asked, "Where are you from, sweetie? What were you doing out there in the rain?"

"I'm from Hummelton," she replied. "It is a little town not too far from here. Soldiers came and killed people." She looked around, and for the first time realized that the room was itself filled with armed men and women. She gave a little shudder before continuing "Ma and Pa and me tried to get away." At this, Allison looked over to Tilly, who nodded her understanding and recruited several others to go search outside for the girl's parents.

"They're not gonna find 'em," Becka said as the door closed. "They didn't come with me. Well," she amended, "they tried to, but when we were climbing the wall some of the soldiers saw us. Da boosted me over, and tried to help Ma up too, but she didn't make it. I called out to them, but they just told me to run, and so I did. I don't know what happened to 'em, but they really sounded scared."

"Well maybe your mother made it after you ran," Allison offered in consolation. "Just because you didn't see her doesn't mean that your father didn't get her over after you ran."

"Maybe," the girl conceded, though she didn't sound hopeful. "But I heard the solders' voices getting closer."

"Well, I am sure they're just fine," Allison cooed. "They were probably just arrested, and once this is all over I bet you and they will find each other and you can go back to your old life together."

Becka nodded silently.

From across the room, Jimmy asked, "So what are we going to do about it?"

"What do you mean?" Thom replied. "You can't possibly think we ought to liberate an entire town, can you? There's not even thirty of us, and you want to take on an army?"

Jimmy shrugged. "Well, when you put it that way, it does sound stupid. But we've got to do something. Look at the girl's feet for gods' sake. She's already been through so much, and we can't very well take her with us east. Do you want us to just leave her here and hope for the best?" He ran a hand through his bushy hair in frustration. "Maybe we can at least get her parents out."

Thom laughed. "So, not liberate the town, but just sneak in, rescue her parents—assuming they're even still alive—and sneak back out without stirring up a massive hornet's next? You're right. That *is* stupid."

When Thom said her parents might be dead Becka stiffened. Allison wrapped her arms around the girl protectively and shot Thom an angry glare. The big man looked embarrassed at his choice of words but didn't seem willing to back down. "I still think it's a stupid idea," he muttered.

"Eh, I've done stupider." Chuck offered in deadpan, surprising everyone in the room. His natural unobtrusiveness had once again caused the others to have forgotten he was there.

"I can confirm this is true," TJ added from his corner, a finger continuing to trace its way down the page of his book as he read. "Our little friend has, on multiple occasions, done what by any objective view would be called stupid." He looked up from his book and concluded, "Not the least of which was when he singlehandedly infiltrated a well defended kobold compound and rescued the four of us from where we were held captive. I believe that was also the time we killed an ogre warlord in Magnus' service. I could be misremembering though." He returned his gaze to his book then added, almost as an afterthought. "Not that I really have an opinion on the matter, for the record."

Thom looked back and forth between the friends, then around the room at the others. "You're serious about this, aren't you?" He threw up his hands in frustration, then stood up and marched out the door and into the rain.

Arms still around Becka, Allison looked over to where her small friend sat quietly. "Ok, Chuckles. I hope you have a plan."

"Not yet," he replied with a smirk, "but just you wait. Just you wait."

CHAPTER 8

The rain continued throughout the following day, but by nightfall had ended. Even so, the skies were still cloudy and the moonlight was wan and diffuse. "Good." Chuck commented from where group huddled outside the town's wall. "It's exactly how Stu promised." He pointed through the darkness to the low palisade that encircled the town of Hummelton, which looked as if it had been built more for defending the townsfolk's gardens from deer than defending the town from assault. It was no surprise that the city had been taken without much difficulty, but it also made getting in, and hopefully out, much easier. Torches blazed at intervals along the wall, but they were haphazardly placed and there was no visible sentry presence.

"I'm embarrassed for them," Tilly muttered. Like Thom, she hadn't been enthusiastic about the rescue mission. When she finally returned, cold and wet, from the unsuccessful search Thom met her outside and filled her in so she was already somewhat agitated when she entered the farmhouse. After a brief, heated exchange over the risks of helping out the girl's parents, Allison ended it by declaring that she and her friends were going to try, and anyone who didn't want to help could stay behind until they got back. The People had, she reminded them again, just shown up of their own volition, and could just as easily leave if they wanted. It was hard to argue with that logic, and while only a half dozen, including Tilly herself, joined the five friends on the mission to Hummelton, the others made ready to provide support if things went awry they needed to make a quick escape. The decision having been made, Stu loped back into the rain to scout the town's perimeter.

"Give me ten minutes," Chuck continued. "If I'm not back by then, either get out of here or bring the cavalry." He paused and smirked. "I'd rather the latter than the former, if you don't mind." The small man darted through the black towards one of the gaps in the torchlight. He scampered over the wall without breaking stride, leaving the others to sit and wait.

"I am kind of hoping that he will need the cavalry," TJ joked. His reagent pouch was open in front of him, and he was ready to cast any number of spells, from a magic shield to a spell of haste to the explosive ball of fire he had almost used on their allies outside Providence City.

"Just leave some for me," Jimmy grunted. He had been in favor of a direct assault from the beginning. For some reason he had taken Becka's story more to heart than the others, and he quickly suggested taking revenge on those who captured her town. Though it wasn't part of the plan, Allison wasn't convinced that he wouldn't charge ahead anyway. His northern blood's fervor was in full evidence.

"Shh," she hushed the two. "TJ, if you just go blowing things up, you're just as likely to hurt Becka's parents and the other townspeople as any of our enemy. And Jimmy, I promise you that soon enough you'll have your fill of battle. It just might not be tonight." She put her hand on his sword arm and held his gaze until he nodded acceptance. Despite the assurances, she knew that if the battle lust overtook him, there would be no holding him back.

Just out of sight, on either side of the group, Stu and Angus each patrolled a flank in case their enemies were out scouting as well. Stu hadn't seen any sentries the prior night, but they wanted to be safe in case the end of the rain had emboldened the soldiers.

"Has it been ten minutes?" TJ asked after a while. "It's got to have been ten minutes" Allison opened her mouth to reply but closed it when she saw Chuck's lithe form slip back over the wall. He darted across the distance and hunkered down in the midst of the group, chest heaving. After taking a moment to catch his breath he announced, "We may have a problem."

"What?" Allison asked. "Are Becka's parents already dead?"

Chuck snorted in reply. "No. That, I'm afraid, would actually *solve* the problem, if you know what I mean. It looks like this isn't going to be a simple grab-and-run. Most, if not all, of the townsfolk have been herded together into a makeshift pen in the middle of the town. They looked a mess, so must have been there through the rain. I don't know what the soldiers have in store for them, but I imagine it's not going to be good. Young and old, they're all out there exposed to the weather." He shook his head. "There's no reason for that other than spite."

"Collective punishment?" Tilly suggested. "Maybe someone knows something and they are doing this to draw out a confession."

"If so," Jimmy replied, "then their situation may get far worse before it gets better. Either no one knows what the soldiers are asking about, or whoever knows is more afraid of sharing the knowledge." His knuckles whitened. "We need to do something."

"Now, wait," objected Olav, one of the People to join the trip who was not from Tilly's unit. "The plan was to rescue the girl's parents, not to liberate the city. In fact, you said we were specifically *not* going to liberate the city. Now it seems like we are?"

Tilly caught Allison's eye and smirked. "Plans change, I guess." She turned to Chuck, who stood patiently. "Tell us everything you saw."

As Chuck described it, the occupying force was small. The hamlet couldn't have had any strategic value, and it was possible that the attackers weren't actually on an official mission at all. Rather, it looked like some soldiers had gotten sick of sleeping in tents while waiting for the army to resume its march west and wanted to sleep in warm, dry, beds. Chuck didn't think they were deserters, as they looked to have settled in, and this was too close to the army's march to be a safe place to hide.

"Tell me about it," Jimmy grumbled. "I'd rather eat a home cooked meal too,"

"Shush," Allison hissed.

"Any soldiers watching the prisoners are giving up a night of relative comfort before resuming the march," Chuck suggested, "so it looks like as many are shirking as possible. There are no more than a half dozen men keeping watch over the corral, and I bet they're the ones who couldn't argue or threaten their way out of it."

"How are they armed?" Jimmy asked.

"They've each got a crossbow in hand and a second nearby, but I don't think they're very worried. The prisoners are shackled at the ankles, so even if they wanted to charge the guards all at once, the chains wouldn't let them.

"How many soldiers in total are there?" Tilly asked.

"Hard to tell," Chuck replied. "Some of the buildings are obviously empty—they're dark and their doors are ajar. Others are obviously occupied, and I could smell the booze wafting out of them. There are several dozen horses, but none are saddled, so I don't know which belong to soldiers and which already live there. Unless we want to wait another day and count heads in the daylight, I'm afraid there's no real way of telling."

A grunt from the darkness startled the group. They drew their weapons and prepared for an attack. A pair of figures emerged from the darkness: Stu escorted a second, unknown man clad in a collection of mismatched armor. He wore the breastplate of an officer and boiled leather on his arms and legs but no helmet. A strip of fabric held a gag inside his mouth and his eyes were wide in terror. Stu gave his captive a shove and the man fell to the ground in front of them.

"Maybe this guy can tell you," Stu observed before disappearing back into the darkness.

Chuck scuttled forward, a dagger held lightly in his hands. "I imagine you know the routine. I will remove the gag, but if you try to call out I will slit your throat. Please don't take offense, but you don't look like the type who would sacrifice his life for his comrades. Am I correct in that assessment?" The captive nodded quickly, his eyes focused on the dagger. "Good." Chuck sliced through the cloth across his mouth and gently extracted the gag. After several seconds of silence, Chuck turned back to Allison and Tilly and said, "I am happy to do the interrogation if you would like, or I can leave it to you."

The two women looked at each other and Allison offered, "I think he will be cooperative enough that we won't need your specialized services. If I am wrong, we will take you up on your offer later." That Chuck had neither any experience as a torturer, nor the stomach to learn on the job was beside the point. So long as their prisoner thought he did, they would learn everything they needed to know.

The man, eyes wide in fear, hissed, "I swear, my Lady! I will tell you anything you wish to know. Just, please don't let him hurt me." His eyes darted around the assembled group looking for any indication that they believed him.

"But of course," Allison began magnanimously. "I believe you completely. Please, share with us what you know about the soldiers occupying that town. So long as you remain truthful, no harm will come to you." She smiled down at him. "Let's start easy. What's your name?"

"It's Tyson," he began hesitantly, but under Allison's friendly gaze he quickly opened up and began almost rambling. The force that had captured the town numbered just under fifty. They were assigned to the very edge of the army's southern flank, and had mostly been left to their own devices. Their only purpose was to keep an eye out for any enemy forces that might come from that direction, and since the start of the campaign, several months ago, they had seen precisely zero enemies. Unsurprisingly, this resulted in their becoming increasingly lax about discipline. When their march brought them to the little town, the decision seemed obvious: enjoy a few days of rest and relaxation before setting back off again. "I'm the newest guy in the unit," he added. "That's why I got stuck on perimeter duty."

As he spoke, Allison peered at him through half closed eyes, letting the cadence of his speech wash over her. She got the sense that he had been forthright. "What about the towns-people?" Allison asked. "How long were you planning on leaving them tied up like animals while you slept in their houses and ate their food? What happens to them when you leave?"

Tyson's body tensed, and only when Chuck cleared his throat did he start to sputter. "It's not up to me," he began, a whine in his voice. "I only follow orders. It's the cap'n who makes the decisions." He took a deep breath. "He's gonna kill 'em all and torch the town. Even though no one is keepin' an eye on us, we never know when a messenger from the high ups might come lookin', and if they learn about what we're doin', it's all our necks. The cap'n plans on reporting that we were attacked. Then, if anyone comes lookin' they won't be surprised at what they find."

"You were going to WHAT?" Allison demanded, launching

herself at him. Only Jimmy's quick reflexes and burly arms kept her from reaching the cowering man.

"I swear, my Lady. It wasn't my idea. But what am I supposed to do but follow orders?"

Allison was shaking in rage and couldn't speak, so Tilly stepped in to continue the questioning. "Why haven't you killed them yet?"

Tyson looked back and forth conspiratorially. "There's treasure hidden around here somewhere." Tilly looked Chuck then back at their prisoner, unsure if was joking or actually stupid enough to believe that one of the townspeople knew where there was buried treasure. Tyson seemed completely earnest, and she clicked her tongue, reassessing their foes. It suddenly seemed more likely that the unit had been sent south not so much to protect the army's flank as to send them where they could do the least harm.

"Your captain," she said. "Does his family have a history of military service?"

"Well ma'am," he answered, "One of the generals is his father. That's why he was trusted with such an important task. They said only he could do it."

By this point Allison had regained her composure, though Jimmy still rested a hand loosely on her shoulder. She asked, "Your captain, the son of a general, was going to burn a town to the ground and kill its inhabitants because he was afraid he'd get in trouble for taking a week or two off from the march? Really?"

"Well, when you put it that way, Lady" he replied, "I guess it sounds kinda funny. But it made perfect sense at the time."

Allison sighed and took a few steps to the side, signaling Tilly and Jimmy to join her. "What a bunch of complete idiots," she offered. "It looks like maybe this will be easier than we thought."

"What should we do with this one?" Chuck called in a cold monotone. Tyson, having forgotten he was there, jumped at the sound and snapped his head around to look wide eyed at the small man.

"My Lady," he stammered pleadingly to Allison. "I've been honest. You promised me."

"Don't worry," she reassured him icily. "We won't kill you in cold blood. For now, you're going to sit here and remain quiet, and I'll figure out what to do with you later." Chuck nodded and faded back into the shadows. To Jimmy she directed, "Gag him again. Let's get this over with."

CHAPTER 9

After Tyson helped Chuck sketch out a map of the town, including where the soldiers slept, they left him tied up beneath a tree. He promised that he would behave himself, and Allison, with her magical intuition, believed him. Even so, no one wished to risk his having a last minute change of heart. He protested the gag at first, but when he learned that the alternative was a whack to the back of the head he acquiesced to both it and the bonds.

Chuck led the other ten attackers to where he had scaled the wall. He went over first to ensure that the coast was still clear, then signaled them with a low whistle. While none were as nimble as Chuck, and Allison—in her heavy metal breastplate—needed a boost from Jimmy, they all made it over without incident. The group split up, with five headed to the cluster of buildings housing the majority of the soldiers and another five to the corral holding Hummelton's populace. Stu hurried to the town's temple, the only building constructed entirely from stone, and quickly climbed to its roof. From there he had a clear shot into nearly all the open areas in town.

Inga rarely left Allison's side, and Cailin did his best to stay away from TJ, so the pair joined Allison, Jimmy, and Chuck to free the captives. The five soon discovered that the sentries had become even more lax in their duties than Tyson described. One sprawled, snoring, across a chair while two others argued drunkenly over a game of dice. Only two of the guards looked alert, keeping a watchful eye on the miserable townspeople as they stood together in hushed conversation. Chuck snuck through the shadows to the one in the chair and slipped a garrote around the man's neck. Though inclined to kill the man outright, under Allison's stern gaze he merely choked him into unconsciousness. Out of the fight was out of the fight, after all, and if it kept a goddess's minion happy, even better.

The two guards who took their job seriously were not as lucky. Because they chatted while watching their prisoners, they didn't notice Jimmy creeping up behind them, his enormous sword held high. Were it not for a young child up well past his bedtime pointing at him and saying, "Look, Mommy!" the pair would never have known how they died. As it was, neither were able to offer more than a vague grunt of surprise before his sword passed through them both in one mighty swing. At the same time, Inga and Cailin assaulted the two gamblers. Reflexes dulled by liquor, they stood on wobbly knees to aid their fallen comrades only to die from swords striking them from behind.

Allison retrieved a ring of keys from one of the fallen soldiers and hurried over to the corral, where she squeezed between two of the rails. She handed the keys to the nearest adult, then immediately began moving through the crowd, looking for any townspeople in need of healing. A general murmur rose among the captives eager to have their own shackles opened but the sight of the giant northerner and his even more giant sword with a finger to his lips quieted them down soon enough. While the Inga and Cailin kept a watch out for other soldiers, Chuck sprinted to the corral's gate and easily picked the lock. After applying a liberal amount of oil to its hinges, he opened the gate with a silent flourish.

"Those of you healthy enough to walk, head toward the town gate," Jimmy hissed. "Anyone who can't move, just sit down and be quiet. We'll be back for you as soon as it's all over." Eager to escape, most of the people limped toward the exit, even those who probably didn't fall into the category of "healthy enough to walk." Even so, everyone held their tongues, including the children, many of whom looked at the soldiers' corpses with wide eyes.

As the captives were being rescued, the other group took up positions outside the buildings in which many of the soldiers were slept. Whether from hubris or incompetence, none of the buildings were guarded, giving the five the opportunity to coax oil lanterns into life. At TJ's signal, four lanterns were thrown into four different buildings, spraying burning oil across the floors. In seconds the buildings were aflame. With a muttered incantation, TJ hurled a ball of magic fire toward another house. The flaming orb flew through a window and exploded, collapsing two walls and dropping the roof onto the soldiers within.

Within moments of the assault's onset, enemies began staggering out of the buildings. Most were without weapons, and some even without pants or shoes. Between Tilly's companions and Stu's arrows, these were killed quickly without even realizing that they were under attack. As he launched arrow after arrow it occurred to Stu that what they were doing to the men wasn't particularly fair. But thinking back to what Tyson said was to happen to the townsfolk steeled his resolve. Having spent much of his youth protecting just such townsfolk from raiders and worse, he understood what needed to be done.

"What is the meaning of this?" a voice from a nearby cottage bellowed. A large, outrageously mustachioed man wearing a well-polished breastplate and helmet emerged, sword in hand. Following him came a handful of other soldiers, each carrying a crossbow and wearing a sword on their belt. Others poured out of houses to either side, and they charged directly at the handful of the People standing amid the bodies of their fallen comrades. Stu's arrows dropped the two leading the charge, but he had to dodge a flight of crossbow bolts shot by the officer's escort. He lost his footing and slid down the steeply angled roof into a ramshackle stack of crates. He landed hard, twisting his right knee and feeling a sharp pain in his lower ribs.

Tilly and her companions closed ranks to fight as a unit, keeping TJ safely behind them. One soldier thrust a sword toward her, and while she easily parried the attack, a second sword followed behind, biting through the leather armor on her left arm and leaving a trail of red in its wake. She gave a grunt of pain and slashed forward with her own sword, but the man had already stepped back and her blade swished harmlessly past his stomach. Just as she made follow with a second swing, a spear thrust out from behind her target. The spear's point was targeted directly at her chest, and having committed to her own attack, she was unable to turn her sword to parry. Cait, however, had herself disengaged with her own opponent, and slapped the spear shaft away with her sword. Tilly had just enough time to recover her footing and step back before the swordsmen once again stepped forward.

The melee soon became too fierce and tight for TJ to risk another explosive burst, so he settled for targeting individual soldiers with weaker magical blasts. The soldiers' crossbows were equally ineffective, so he didn't need to worry about being turned into a pincushion. While his magical attacks kept them from being overrun, his friends were hard pressed. The officer and his guards marched toward them leisurely, a smile across his face. "Give 'em hell, boys!" He cried, brandishing his own sword over his head. TJ targeted the man with several balls of force, but after the first collided with the man's breastplate two of his guards stepped forward to absorb the subsequent blasts with their shields. Knowing that they would soon be overwhelmed, TJ called a wall of fire into being between the two groups. The soldiers facing them fell back as magical flames burned exposed flesh and set their clothes afire.

"To me! To me!" TJ shouted into the night, as the five used the flames as cover to back away, hopeful that the other group had already dealt released the prisoners and could come to their aid. The wall of flames was only ten feet wide, and while it incapacitated the first line of soldiers, once the others had recovered from their surprise they could just go around it.

As if on cue, the officer appeared from their left, leading his men in a charge toward the retreating group. Olav, on Tilly's left fell to a lucky spear thrust, and TJ and the others were quickly surrounded. The attackers' faces made it clear that they would not be taking prisoners; too many of their friends had been slain that night for them to offer quarter. In desperation, TJ tapped into what was left of his flagging power and erected an invisible barrier of force around the four of them. A sword struck out only to rebound and the surprised soldier lost his grip. Cait took the opportunity to stab at the suddenly disarmed foe, but her blade was similarly turned aside. With both strikes TJ felt the reverberation all through his body. He knew he provided them with only a temporary respite, and that their only real hope was for the others to rescue them. If they didn't? Well, he wouldn't go down without taking all his enemies with him.

It didn't take long for the soldiers to notice that each strike against the force wall visibly pained the wizard. They began hammering at it with sword and shield, and Tilly murmured, "So how long can you keep that up?"

"Not forever," he replied with a grimace.

As TJ's strength flagged, the barrier shrank inward. Where there had been enough space for Tilly, Cait, and Afner to assume comfortable, en garde stances there was now barely room to stand without brushing shoulders. "Or even much longer at all," he heaved. "I hope you have made peace with your gods." The three others grunted their replies.

Up. Down. Up. Down. Blades rose and fell, sending TJ to a knee in exhaustion. He looked up to see a blade fall backwards out of the soldier's grasp rather than forward into the shield. The man collapsed, an arrow in his back. Only after a second man fell did the soldiers realize they were being fired upon. "There!" one cried, pointing at where Stu leaned against the church's wall, one of his legs dangling uselessly. Two soldiers raised their heavy shields and charged, deflecting the arrows targeted at their comrades. Unable to strike killing blows, Stu instead sent an arrow low, pinning one of the men's feet to the ground and sending him sprawling as his momentum carried him forward but his boot refused to move. Without time to shoot at the second attacker, Stu raised his bow to ward off the charging man's strike. Before his sword could fall, however, Allison stepped out from around another corner and let loose a blast of concentrated, holy energy. The soldier was lifted off his feet and slammed headfirst into the wall. Unconscious or dead, he wouldn't be getting up soon.

TJ's barrier had almost completely dissipated. Sword strokes had begun to penetrate the barrier before slowing to a halt as if they were cutting into chilled molasses. Beside the wizard, the others raised their swords and prepared for one last violent clash. A loud keening wail heralded a large shape barreling across the open ground. Jimmy crashed headlong into the group of soldiers still hacking at the barrier, sending them all tumbling to the ground. As he scrambled back up, Cailin and Inga added their own battle cries to the din, and what had looked to become an exercise in butchery became a pitched battle between evenly matched sides. Swords rebounded from shields as each tried to break through the other's defenses.

"Throw down your weapons, men!" a cried the captain's voice. No one let down their guard, but the two sides reduced the fury of their attacks. "I said, we surrender! Throw down your weapons!" the cry came again, and this time the soldiers slowly backed away and one by one dropped their swords in surrender, all the while looking for their captain. Not far away knelt their leader, Chuck behind him with a knife pressed against his neck.

Once the soldiers had dropped their weapons, Allison dashed to where Olav lay, but found that he had died from his wounds during the fight. After saying a silent prayer for the dead, she turned to those she could still help. Stu's injuries were the worst, but by channeling her magic into both his knee and his ribs he was soon walking without pain. Jimmy had taken a slash to his forehead, and Cait a stab to the thigh. Both were quickly fixed as well. While Allison tended to the wounded, Inga jogged toward the town gates to let the townspeople know that it was safe to return to their homes.

The soldiers let themselves be bound hand and feet and only then did Allison inspect them for wounds. When any life-threatening injuries were dealt with, they were herded into the corral that until recently held the townspeople. Including the officer, there were fewer than a dozen of the town's occupiers still alive. While his men looked dejected and defeated, the mustachioed older man continued to radiate bile and outrage. "You will pay for this! You don't know who I am. You will be hunted to the ends of the earth for this!" His angry cries were almost uniformly ignored by the townspeople and their liberators alike; they had more important things to do. Most had not eaten a crumb since being captured, and the only drink they had received was from whatever rain they were able to trap from the prior day's storm.

Volunteers carried around buckets of water from the town's well and passed out what was left of their stockpiled food. The buildings that had been set alight weren't salvageable, mostly because of how hot the lantern oil burned. Luckily the town's structures were spread out enough that there was no risk of the fires spreading, as everyone was too exhausted from the ordeal to fight a fire anyway.

Although the immediate danger had passed, Allison was unwilling to rest until she had found Becka's parents and reassured them that the girl had survived her flight. Returning to the corral, she first checked on the few who had not fled through the city gates. As she provided them what healing they needed, she questioned them on the pair's whereabouts. None could offer more guidance than pointing toward the town's gates, though one older woman claimed not to have seen them at all.

"Don't look at me like that, girlie," the crone grumbled when Allison gave her a doubtful look. "This town isn't so big I don't know who all my neighbors are. You're talkin' about Jennie and Willis, and I was the woman at both of their births. If I say they weren't here, they weren't here."

Her claim was borne out when the last of the townspeople returned through the gate. Everyone agreed that the pair were not with the group that snuck out during the fight, and no one remembered seeing them at all during the ordeal. Looking at the still-burning buildings and fearing the worst, Allison started circling through town.

"Jennie!" Allison shouted, her voice going hoarse. "Willis! Where are you?" The sound of coughing from behind one of the houses closest to the town wall pulled her up short. She crept around the back and found a dirty, disheveled woman crouching protectively in front of a prone figure, her grimy face illuminated by the flames from a nearby house.

"Stay back," the woman snarled. Behind her, the body twitched slightly. Allison's intuition told her he did would not live much longer without treatment. "You ain't gonna touch him again."

Allison raised her hands in supplication. "It's okay. My name is Allison. Are you Jennie?" She inclined her head toward the body on the ground. "Is that Willis?"

"I am, and he is, and you ain't gonna hurt him again." Jennie waved the knife back and forth to punctuate her assertion.

"Don't worry," Allison cooed. "No one's going to hurt either of you. In fact, I'm a priestess, and I can heal him." She paused a heartbeat. "We found Becka. Your daughter is safe."

"Becka?" The woman's eyes glistened.

"Yes," Allison replied. "She found us and told us what happened and we came straight here. She was very brave."

Jennie dropped the knife and threw herself at Allison's feet, sobbing unreservedly. Allison let her do so for a few seconds before gently stepping away and approaching Willis. The man had been brutally beaten, and his skin was covered with burns. Allison touched him gently on his forehead and let healing power rush into the injured man. The burns healed before her eyes, leaving only the faintest of pink scars. He met her gaze and gave her a wan smile, but she knew that while she had healed the wounds to his body, those to his spirit wouldn't fade as easily.

Allison looked back to Jennie, who answered the unspoken question. "After we got Becka over the wall, the solders beat him up pretty bad. They said they weren't done with us yet, and locked us into a room in one of the houses they were using. Didn't bother letting us out once the fire started either. As we were trying to get out Willis' legs gave out and got himself burned, but luckily I was able to drag him out over here." She crawled back over to where her husband lay, and cradled his head in her lap.

"Well, you can both rest now," Allison replied, "and Becka will be here by morning."

"Thank you, Lady," Jennie said. "May the Goddess bless you."

Allison smiled back, then left the pair to themselves and returned to join the others. She found her friends near the corral, standing in front of their captives and discussing what to do with them while several of the townsfolk looked on angrily. "We should hang them," suggested Cait. "They're thieves and murderers, and deserve no less." Cailin nodded, from time to time glancing at where his sister had been wounded.

"It's no less than Olav deserves," he said, referring to the man who had been killed by the spear.

"I don't know," Allison replied, feeling queasy at the thought of executing the men outright. "Tyson said the captain made all the decisions, and they were just following along. Just following orders isn't a real defense,"—She'd learned that in European History—"but let's be honest. These folks aren't the critical thinking type. I imagine that's why they ended up with this miserable officer."

During it all, the captain continued to spew vitriol at anyone and everyone nearby, either uncaring or unaware that they held his fate in their hands. "Tyson? Is he the bastard who ratted us out?" The man sputtered in response to Allison's comment. "He'll pay for this along with the rest of you! Just you wait!" Allison was much more ambivalent about the thought of execution for him.

"Ok, fatty, that's enough" Jimmy said, giving the man's booted foot a light kick. The officer's eyes bulged at the insult but his voice petered off. "You seem to have a lot to say," Jimmy continued. "What do *you* think we should do with the lot of you?"

"I demand that you release me immediately! My uncle is the army's supreme commander and he has the ear of the great wizard Magnus himself. When he learns of what you've done there will be nowhere you can hide from his wrath. The great one himself will track you down and exact retribution!" Chuck noticed that one of the bound soldiers rolled his eyes in spite of himself and his precarious position. It seemed that neither news of his connections nor his willingness to invoke them were a surprise to his soldiers.

"Well, that's one option," Allison offered. She looked at the others as if seriously asking their opinions on his suggestion. "We could release you to the tender mercies of the good townspeople that you until very recently had chained up like animals. I wonder which they find more compelling,"—She stroked an imaginary beard—"your threats or their revenge?" Though they kept their silence, the townsfolk's faces made clear what they thought of Allison's question. Though the officer continued to glare his defiance, the suggestion clearly rattled his men. "Or," she offered nonchalantly, "perhaps we could just strip you naked, tie you up, and put the town to the torch. I could swear that I've heard that idea bandied about as well."

The captain appeared ready to protest again, but TJ knelt next to him, his eyes flickering with arcane power. "Magnus is not the only wizard worth fearing. Let him find us. It will save us the trouble of hunting him down before we kill him."

The overweight officer looked back and forth between TJ Allison for some indication that it was a joke.

"You're all mad, aren't you?" He shook his head. "Fine, we give in."

Tilly barked a laugh. "Give in? Even in defeat, you city folk are arrogant." She looked to Allison. "The choice is up to you, Lady, but I say we kill them all and be done with it. As Cait said, it's no less than they deserve. Now, if you will excuse me, I will return to our camp and let the others know we were successful. We will be back around sunrise, and will bring the girl Becka with us." The young woman turned on her heel and disappeared into the dark, leaving the officer to stare after her, mouth agape.

CHAPTER 10

Unsurprisingly, Allison did not in fact issue an order to execute the captives. The boys had fallen into the habit of deferring to her leadership, and Tilly's comrades continued to look upon her with a certain amount of awe, so while she was pretty sure that the People and at least one of her companions would have followed such an order, she was completely sure she didn't have the stomach to issue it. Rather, she directed the soldiers be shackled as the townsfolk had been, assigned Cait and Cailin to sentry duty, and had everyone else catch a few hours of sleep.

The captive soldiers gave their guards no trouble overnight; the siblings took the assignment seriously instead of gambling and drinking the night away. This turned out to be lucky for the prisoners, as not long after the rest of the town had gone to sleep several men whose houses had been ransacked by the invaders crept out of their houses with murder on their minds. When the townsfolk saw that the pair would not back down even in the face of their righteous belligerence, they withdrew to their houses, grumbling and swearing oaths of vengeance.

When they woke, the friends found that Tilly and the others had returned, and Becka had already been reunited with her parents. Tilly reported that the girl still seemed out of sorts and anxious over her ordeal, but had been smothered by hugs from not only her immediate family, but many other townspeople. Word had spread that it had been her bravery that brought their liberators to the town, and her neighbors were effusive in their gratitude. There was even talk of naming a holiday after her.

"I see the vermin still live," Tilly observed when Allison and the others met her outside the corral. "Have you decided what to do with them?"

The friends had discussed that very thing at length earlier before going to sleep, and they all agreed that killing them was out of the question. Allison worried that some of the People, such as Thom, thought her too soft because of her insistence on helping Becka. Because of this, they decided that Jimmy should give the order, since he was a veteran of many battles and was less likely to appear squeamish. "Yes." The big man announced. "We are going to strip them of their possessions and send them on their way. They can return to the captain's uncle if they want."

The officer, who had regained his bluster during the night, shook with indignation. "You can't do that to us!" he cried, mustache flapping wildly. "We'll never make it back to our forces alive without weapons or armor. And even if we did, how am I supposed to explain that my entire company was killed or captured out from under me by a handful of barbarians? I'll lose my command!"

"Actually," Chuck countered, "you're more likely to lose your head. I've heard that your friend Magnus is not terribly fond of those who fail him, and if I were to pick a word to describe what happened here 'failure' would be a good one. I don't think your dear uncle is going to be able to shield you from the wizard's wrath." The officer's eyes grew wide as the truth of Chuck's words settled in. Chuck continued, "My suggestion would be to go south, not north. Flee and hope that those of the Arcanum never even think of you again. Of course, if he ever does learn of what happened here, well, how did you put it? 'The great one himself will track you down ... and exact retribution.'" Chuck delivered the last two sentences in a rough approximation of the officer's own voice.

Upon hearing this last bit the soldiers shackled alongside him had had enough. Up to that point they hoped their leader's connections to the army's upper echelons would keep them safe. Seeing him dissolve into a sobbing mess changed their perspectives completely. Each began making their own cases for why they should be treated differently and how they were unwitting pawns of their evil captain. Several went so far as to sneer at him, accusing him of making the whole uncle thing up.

"Oh shush, all of you," Allison scolded in irritation. "If you were so put upon you shouldn't have been treating the people here like cattle to be milked and slaughtered. You're lucky that we're the ones deciding your fate and not anyone else. If it were up to our friends, you'd already be hanging from a gibbet. And right now I'm beginning to wonder if that might be a better choice."

Her outburst silenced the group, except for the captain, who continued to sniffle. Their captives now tried to make themselves look as quiet and innocent as possible. It was both ridiculous to see and further proof that these were among the least useful, least wanted soldiers in the army. They, along with their well-connected but otherwise inept leader had been sent well away from where they could do any actual harm. It was just dumb luck that the people of Hummelton bore the brunt of their abuse. Inga took over guarding the captives, giving Cait, Cailin, and the others from the farmhouse the opportunity to sleep. Meanwhile, the townspeople in their gratitude arranged a feast for their liberators. Allison, refreshed from her nap, took a second pass through the townsfolk, healing any remaining scrapes or bruises left over from their imprisonment.

Later that day Thom oversaw the funeral preparations for Olav. They laid him to rest just outside the town's walls in the manner of their people: first burying the body then covering the plot with a small cairn of stones. As nomads, they had no walled cemeteries to protect the bodies of the dead from scavengers. The combination of digging and covering assured their loved ones the dignity of a final rest safe from hungry jaws. Olav was buried in his armor, his hands holding the hilt of the sword that ran the length of his body. Allison and Jimmy watched the ceremony from a short distance away, not wanting to intrude, but feeling a need to be there for their fallen comrade. When the last words were spoken over the grave Tilly asked Allison deliver final rites on behalf of the Goddess. Despite never before attending a funeral in this world, the words came unbidden to her lips.

Chuck used the time to search through the captain's belongings and discovered a bound sheaf of documents. His primary interest was to acquire copies of any papers with official signatures or seals to copy for forgeries. He quickly found a travel pass, the officer's official commission to the army, and the orders sending him and his unit south.

Captain Marston:

The quality in which you have consistently performed your duties, as well as the overall quality of soldiers under your command, has been brought to the attention of the Army's highest levels. After much discussion among the general staff about which tasks are most fitting for you and those you lead, you are hereby reassigned from the force's main body.

In recognition of your singular ability, you are hereby directed to take your unit to Valewards province on the army's southern flank. There, you are to search out and destroy any and all enemies. You will maintain this position until you have received further instructions from me.

Please believe me when I say that there are no other soldiers and no other officer to whom I would trust this mission. Your presence on our flank is critical to ensuring the success of our campaign as a whole. I have every confidence that our expectations for you will be met.

General Dmitri Manev

General of Arcanum Forces

By the time Chuck had gotten to the end of the orders, he could barely control his laughter. "Their expectations?" he said aloud between snorts. "I'm betting that what happened tonight was entirely consistent with their expectations. He had never before seen such a wonder of doublespeak, and only wished he had a wall on which to frame it.

He emerged from the house to find his friends relaxing

around a communal fire pit. They were chatting away with some of the town's elders and fielding questions from curious children bent on emulating their new heroes. Some were swinging long branches and yelling battle cries like Jimmy, whereas some pretended to cast spells to "catch the bad guys on fire." A number of the elder girls, Becka included, eyed Tilly as she prowled around giving orders. While battle-tested priestesses like Allison were uncommon, the woman who walked, fought, and gave orders like a man was almost unimaginable. At first the young woman ignored their curious gazes as she rushed to and fro, it wasn't long before she found herself surrounded by curious young women full of questions.

Chuck flopped down on an empty chair and put his feet up on a log to warm them by the fire. "Find anything good, Chuckles?" Jimmy asked.

The small man made a sour face and replied, "You know I hate it when you call me that." Allison, surprised by the comment, caught Jimmy's eye and he shrugged absently. The little man's face quickly shifted back its normal friendly coun-tenance and he answered cheerfully, "All the stuff I could have hoped for, and more!"

"Really, that good?" Jimmy leaned forward in his seat, eager to hear about the haul.

"No, not really," Chuck giggled, "but given what a waste of ribbons that guy is I wasn't really hoping for much. I found some stuff that might be of use if I need to sneak us in some-where, but also," he paused and pulled a stack of envelopes out of his shirt with a flourish. "These!" The packet of papers was tied neatly with a woman's hair ribbon and the perfume in which they had been doused was obvious, even over the scent of woodsmoke.

"Love letters?" Stu rolled his eyes. "The last thing I want to know about is what kind of woman would fall for such a cretin."

If Chuck was offended by Stu's sudden vehemence he didn't show it. "Come now, Stu! Imagine the blackmailing possibilities with such details!" His gaze fell out of focus as he thought about the potential. "But no, that's not what's interesting. We don't need the money even if it were. This is far more useful."

"How so?" TJ asked, startling the others. He often sank into silence as deep as Stu's and it was never clear when he was paying attention.

"Well, my dear wizard," he said magnanimously, "it turns out that our friend over yonder was only telling part of the truth. The lord high general is not in fact his uncle, but rather the father of his sweet paramour, Emmaline." Jimmy opened his mouth to ask a question but Chuck raised his hand to stop him. "What does this have to do with us, you are no doubt asking. Well it appears that while '*My true love captain Alfred*,'" he said the title in a sing-song voice, "may have been banished to the outer reaches of the content, his lady keeps in touch relentlessly. And," he added, "she has joined her exalted father on his campaign west." Realization had begun to dawn on his friend's faces, but he was on a roll and concluded his thoughts anyway. "The most recent letter was dated less than a week ago. She drones on and on about love and beauty and blah blah blah, but within that bundle of mush she makes sure he knows exactly where to send his replies."

The others leaned forward, suddenly eager to hear the rest of Chuck's news. "It turns out that dear old daddy has a very important meeting quite far away from where the bulk of his army waits. According to her letter, he will be traveling light and fast, and, most importantly, without many guards. She is feeling very put out about it, you know. The meeting is to be held behind the southern flank of the army—only a couple days' light travel from here—and she was not invited to go along."

"So let me get this straight," Allison said. "The lightly-protected high commander of the Arcanum's army is but a stone's throw away from where we now sit?"

The friends' eyes, even TJ's, lit up.

Jimmy gave a toothy grin. "I think that maybe we should pay him a visit."

CHAPTER 11

According to his daughter's letter, the Arcanum general would be meeting a contact about two days' ride from Hummelton. The meeting was set to occur any day now, so rather than enjoying the hospitality of the townsfolk, the group set off immediately, following a map Chuck found in the general's possessions. Allison was surprised that none of the People returned to Olav's grave before leaving, or even talked of their lost comrade as they prepared to march.

"Death is common among our people," Thom explained to her as they rode. "In fact, it is a blessing that we lost only a single man in the raid. That is why I opposed it from the outset. Just because death is common doesn't mean it was wise to go looking for it needlessly."

The people of Hummelton had decided to pack up their things and head south and west, at least for the time being. Their walls were obviously not up to repelling even the most inept attackers, and even if their defenses could be strengthened, there weren't enough men of fighting age to stand guard. The young women's adoration of Tilly and her braggadocio did not replace military training; it would take months or even years of training before they were ready to defend their town. The friends left their wagon for the townspeople to use to transport their goods as most of their original supplies, including the ale, had been used up. They also expected to be moving through rougher terrain to avoid enemy patrols, and the wagon wasn't built for such duty.

"I wonder what the soldiers will end up doing," Allison mused. In their haste to reach the general's rendezvous in time they hadn't had the opportunity to strip them of armor and send them on their way. "With the townsfolk all leaving, do you think they'll stay put in Hummelton? Or do you think they'll run south like you suggested?"

Chuck looked ready to make a snarky comment, but the earnest look on Allison's face made him hold his tongue. On Allison's other side, Jimmy gave a subtle shake of his head. "No," the small man finally said. "I doubt that they are just going to leave the town to the soldiers. I'm sure they'll figure out something to do with them."

Allison nodded, not sure she liked the tone of his voice but let it go.

Stu and Angus had once again ranged ahead to break the trail, as the farther east they went the more likely they were to run into enemy soldiers. No one worried about being ambushed—who would imagine so small a group would march against the Arcanum's forces—but it would be just as bad to encounter a company of regular soldiers headed to the front as reinforcements and have to explain why they themselves were going east. From time to time, as his power allowed, TJ would enter a trance to scry ahead. Together, the scouts and the wizard guided them successfully between enemy units.

Rain fell again that night, but they made cold camp nonetheless, not wanting to risk any Arcanum troops seeing their fire. This resulted in a group of damp, aching travelers the following morning. Spirits rose with the sun, but by evening a malaise set in again. While no one argued about taking their turn at sentry duty, there was a little grumbling when Tilly handed out assignments. She reminded them that no one had forced them to come on the journey, and they could similarly leave any time their honor allowed. The none-too-subtle guilt trip made Allison uncomfortable, and she said so.

"Whether or not you feel uncomfortable is beside the point. After what you did for us I would follow you to the very ends of the world, to death itself." Many of the others echoed that sentiment loudly, and the more vocal grumblers quieted down. Even so, Jimmy insisted that he, Chuck, and Stu each join one of the turns at watch that evening. He didn't think any of those who came on the quest would do anything rash, but half of them—including Thom, Tilly's second—had already demonstrated that they were willing to choose a different path from the others.

Near sundown the following day Stu was able to point out landmarks the map said were close to the rendezvous point. Allison urged haste, as there was no guarantee that the meeting would last very long. The general would only have traveled that distance for a great need, but it could be something as simple as a "for your hands only" delivery from one important person to another. If so, the general would immediately return north.

Allison only agreed to stop pushing forward when full darkness had fallen and even Tilly urged caution. "If a horse steps in a hole and breaks a leg," she argued, "not only are we down a mount, but the animal's noise could give us away. The last thing we need is to betray our presence when we are so close to our quarry."

Allison dismounted, then dropped to the ground limply, leaning back against a tree. "So close. I pray to the Goddess that we don't miss this opportunity." After two days of hurried marches she, along with most of the others, were both physically and mentally exhausted. "Who has the map?"

Thom waved at her from across the clearing where he sat. "I do, Lady Allison." He stood and walked to join her, then hunkered down and spread the parchment across the ground. Clouds covered the moon and most of the stars, so they took the risk of lighting a lantern. Angus, taking a turn back at the camp, stepped over to point out the features he and Stu had noticed.

"There, Lady, is the range of hills that we saw to the south." His finger traced the lines of the map as he identified each in turn. "The forestland visible to the east lies here, perhaps another few day's travel. And, of course, Hummelton is marked here. That puts tonight's camp right in this area, give or take."

"Give or take?" Allison scrunched her nose.

"Unfortunately, yes. I have no way of knowing how accurate this map is. One would think an officer's maps would be of high quality, but Captain Alfred himself hardly inspired much confidence. For all we know, this is a carnival trickster's treasure map." He shrugged apologetically. "Add to that the fact that we are using love letters to tell us where to go. It ought to be over here," he pointed to the X they had drawn on the map with the villagers' advice, "but it could be anywhere within fifty miles."

"Including possibly just over the next rise?"

"Yes, including possibly just over the next rise. Just as Stu and I have been roving ahead, they no doubt have scouts of their own looking for potential threats. We find ourselves in a dangerous situation."

"Speaking of which," Thom said quietly enough for only Allison and Angus to hear. "Are you sure that you want to go through with this? You have to know the victory at Hummelton was a fluke. The only reason it succeeded was because you faced an unprepared, under-trained, and undisciplined foe. This general is going to have much better protection, and you won't be able to just walk in and capture him. Is this attack so important that you are ready to lose men and women on it?"

Allison held his gaze. "What do you suggest? From what I remember, you were impressed by my plan to just march east until we find Magnus and then kill him. What happened to that?"

He snorted. "Part of me didn't really think you were being serious. I figured that you actually had more of a plan than that, even if it was incomplete. The other part of me was drunk and it seemed like a good joke. Now that I'm sober, I've found my sense of humor has fled me. These are good people you command, Lady. Do not throw their lives away on a whim."

Angus looked back and forth between Thom and Allison, not

willing to get into the middle of their argument. Tilly appeared from the darkness and stood over the three of them. "I've had just about enough of this, Thom," she started. "I made it clear from the beginning that no one was being forced to come east. Some took me up on that offer and are still camped outside Providence City waiting for the Warlord to make his decision. We all have our own codes of honor, and no one will judge or jeer if you decide to return home." She raised her voice and turned back to the center of the camp. "But let me say this as plainly as I can. I will hear no more of this complaining. Anyone who stays with us *will* follow orders. I will not tolerate another incident like at the farmhouse. Had you all been with us, Olav would still walk among us. You are either with us or not, and if you are not, I expect you to leave at first light."

She spoke the last sentence directly to Thom, who stared her down, red-faced, for several long seconds before nodding and spitting, "Yes, *captain*." He stood and stalked off into the darkness.

Allison looked to Angus, who didn't meet her eyes, then up at Tilly. The other woman grimaced and explained, "Don't worry about Thom. He just needs some time to settle down. This isn't the first time we've had this sort of discussion and in the end he always gets things sorted out in his head. Now let me see that map ..."

As the evening progressed, the friends each settled into their own routines. Chuck, as always, found a tree with large branches and settled in to sleep. Not for the first time, Allison shook her head at how easily he contorted himself to do so. TJ retreated into the caverns of his own mind, if not pondering the great mysteries of the universe, at least perusing the tomes of knowledge stored within.

Jimmy worked through a series of limbering and combat routines, which he explained was necessary on those days he did not actually get to fight anyone. "Wouldn't want to get rusty, after all. It's been days since I stabbed someone, and that is the sort of thing that if you don't practice you lose!" He laughed at his joke and was joined in his mirth by most of the People, though Allison didn't really think it was funny. Whether it was because she played a healer or still saw herself as a fifteen-year-old girl, she still felt a little guilty about the soldier she had smited to keep him from attacking Stu. When the fight was finished and they looked for wounded, they found he had broken his neck.

Of Stu, there was no sign. After sharing some of their cold dinner, he had once again strode off into the darkness. Silent as usual, he had left no indication of when he would return. Though she had faith in all her friends' talents, she still felt anxious not having him in sight. It was, she reflected, also part of the healer thing, in that if her job was to keep them all alive, she could not actually do her job if they were not around. Perhaps it was also that she seemed to be the only one focused on getting them all home.

Sighing to herself, Allison took one last look around the campsite before settling into her bedroll and closing her eyes. Doubts plagued her thoughts and sleep was slow in coming.

CHAPTER 12

When the group rose the following morning neither Stu nor Thom had returned to the camp. None of the sentries posted overnight reported any sign of either, though, at least with Stu, they acknowledged that he could have slipped in and out without their noticing.

"Is that supposed to make us feel good or bad?" Jimmy asked over breakfast. "It's great that he is that talented, but if it is all the same to you, I would rather the folks keeping us from getting killed in the night be even better."

"Well, look on the bright side," Chuck replied. "Worst case scenario, he's out killing all our enemies while their scouts come in and kill all of us. Or rather,"—he sniggered—"all of you, since we have already established that I am immune to such nighttime chaos. Then their guy and our guy Stu can duke it out while I loot all the corpses and get out of here."

"You talk tough, little man," Allison teased. "But you could have left us any number of times over the last several months, particularly during that last bout of nighttime chaos. You are going to be here with us until the end."

"That is only because I like you," he replied magnanimously, eliciting a guffaw from Jimmy. "I reserve the right to stop liking you, and if I do, I and my well-earned loot are out of here." He paused a moment, looking thoughtful. "Oh, and if I ever start actively *hating* you, then I'll take all of *your* well-earned loot with me when I go!" He nodded to punctuate his statement.

Allison shook her head in mock exasperation, though part of her wondered how much of what he said really was just teasing. He had been the first to show real signs of his game personality, and his out-of-the-blue claim the other day that he hated the nickname Chuckles concerned her. As far as personalities went, neither Stu nor Chuck were team players, a fact that weighed heavily on her mind while the archer was missing from camp, as either could disappear without a trace. She had fewer concerns that the other two boys might turn aside from the quest. Jimmy was completely at home with the People, and would stay with the group just for the fighting and the excitement of the journey. His complaint about not having been able to stab anyone recently rung far more true than he may have meant it.

And TJ? Of the four she had been closest to him before all this started. They had been best friends, spending more time with each other than with the rest of their friends combined. But over time he had become less and less concerned with the world around him and more drawn into himself. She thought he would follow through the quest until the end as well, if only for the opportunity to continue to hone and test his magical abilities. It was, however, cold consolation; while his physical and arcane presence was reassuring for the sake of their task, his emotional and social distance became harder to take every day.

Angus had been spared a nighttime watch so that he could leave before dawn to scout the surrounding terrain. Before they broke camp they wanted to be sure that they weren't walking straight into the middle of an armed encampment. An hour after sunrise he loped back into camp to report. "I found no sign of the enemy nearby, though we're getting close. As the sun rose this morning there was smoke wafting far off in the distance. It could be from a homesteader's hearth, but if it's from our target they're at least a half day's ride, longer if we go on foot. Since it was only their smoke that gave them away, our cold camp probably means their scouts have no idea we're here."

"Assuming they are sending out scouts at all," mused Tilly. "How hard would you look for enemies if you were deep behind the lines of your own invading army? I bet they will only have perimeter sentries, and they'll be no more vigilant than the ones we saw in Hummelton."

"I agree," Jimmy said. "If they were worried about an attack, their commander would never have gone off with as small a guard as his daughter's letter indicated. He would have moved in force, or made whomever he is meeting come to him. I doubt they'll be dicing and drinking, but I'm sure they'll be more worried about what's on tomorrow's breakfast menu than being attacked."

"Good." Allison nodded. "We should start to move. Not too quickly, though, and I want another scout to ride with Angus since Stu is still missing. Even if the high general came with a small entourage, whoever he was meeting may have more men under their own command. We are few, and as much honor as dying in glorious battle may convey upon you and your families, I would rather avoid such honors for the time being."

"Speaking of which," TJ interrupted, startling everyone. "In addition to Stu, we appear to be missing another of our fellows. In particular, it's the one who also expressed an unwillingness to earn said honors at this juncture. I am curious, Captain, as to whether you have any insight into his whereabouts." He nodded to Tilly and stood quietly, waiting for her answer.

"Yeah, well," she began hesitantly. "Like I said, he has a short temper, and this isn't anything he hasn't done before." At TJ's raised eyebrow she continued, "Of course he's never stormed off when we were this close to battle. It's usually when we have had down time and he hasn't had a good fight to burn off some energy."

"Um, just how often *does* he do this?" Chuck asked. "You make it seem like this is a pretty regular occurrence. Just how often can someone do that and still be considered officer material? Growing up in Freeport, you pulled something like that, you woke up with your throat slit and that would have been that." He noticed a look of surprise on Allison's face and he shrugged at her. "I didn't have the luxury of growing up in a temple, *Lady Allison*. The streets are a rough place to live." She raised her hands in surrender and looked back to Tilly.

"Yes, well," she began. "Luckily, my people do *not* live in that festering wound of a city, and no one ever 'wakes up with their throat slit' as you so casually put it. Thom, while volatile, is an excellent warrior and a tribute to his family. In fact, his volatility is exactly what makes him such an excellent warrior, so his outbursts have sometimes been overlooked. Perhaps we have been too soft on him over the years, but that is something to be taken up when we finish this task and return home to our people." She took a deep breath. "In the meanwhile, we will just have to move on without him. If he plans to return, he will. If he instead chooses to return home, then he is no longer our concern and we can forget about him. Either way, I suggest we break camp and get moving. The day is not getting any younger."

Tilly surveyed the camp. "You heard what I had to say last night," she called out. "This is the time to make your choice. You are either with us to the end or you leave now, and I expect all who stay to follow my commands and those of Lady Allison. Are there any who wish to leave?" Tilly counted ten heartbeats, during which none of her comrades made a move. She smiled and nodded her gratitude. "I thank you for your faith in my abilities and your own. Now, let's get moving!"

Along with Angus, a wiry young woman named Ashley left camp after they each hastily swallowed a couple slices of salt pork. They jogged off on foot, leaving their horses behind so that an errant hoof clop or nicker would not give them away. About twenty minutes later the rest of the group broke camp and followed on horseback. They set a leisurely pace so as not to get too close to their enemy before getting more information from the scouts. They were all too aware of how few they numbered, and much preferred attacking at night when the number differential would make less of a difference. Just as at Hummelton, the nighttime sentries could be dealt with individually first. Then, with the element of surprise, they could trick the enemy into thinking the attacking force was much larger than it was.

They rode in silence, each lost in their own thoughts about the upcoming fight. They all knew that Thom was right—they had been extremely lucky in the last battle, losing only Olav in combat. It was unrealistic to believe that this next fight would be as easy. It was a certainty that at this time the next day the group would be smaller. The only question was, who would continue to ride and who would be left behind? Each promised themselves that it wouldn't be they who fell in battle, but not all promises can be kept.

The sun was well past its zenith when Ashley, panting heavily and covered in dirt and scratches, emerged from some scrub. Tilly raised her arm signaling a halt, and she, along with Allison and Jimmy, slid off their horses to meet the scout.

"What news?" Tilly asked curtly, and handed Ashley a water skin. The other woman took a deep drink and wiped her mouth with the back of her hand before speaking.

"We found the camp, and they are closer than we thought. No more than five miles away. There are sentries posted, and scouts ranging out. Even now you may have come closer than is prudent for daytime. There is a glen about two miles away where we can wait until nightfall." She handed the skin back to Tilly, who, after a brief glance to Allison, nodded her head.

"Good work," she acknowledged. "Lead the way."

Ashley led them due south into a band of trees, almost directly away from where the general's camp was situated. The brush thickened around them and they were forced to dismount and lead their horses. Twenty minutes later, the foliage thinned and the group led their horses into a clearing no more than fifty yards across. The ruined foundations of a house lay in a haphazard pile, suggesting that the open space was not a natural feature of the woods. From behind this pile Thom emerged, dragging a bound and blindfolded Angus, a dagger held to the scout's neck. Thom's face bore a cruel grin and his eyes glinted madly. Ashley looked at Tilly apologetically, but made no move to leave the group or defend herself. "I'm sorry," she murmured.

Jimmy immediately drew his giant blade, and the others in the party followed suit. The large man made to step forward but Allison tugged on his sleeve, holding him back. "Don't," she murmured. "He hasn't killed Angus yet, which means we may yet be able to talk him out of this."

"What is the meaning of this?" Tilly took several steps forward. "Quit hiding behind a captive and let Angus go. You dishonor yourself and your clan!"

"I'll tell you what the meaning of this is," Thom called back. "You don't deserve to lead, and you never have. Because of your adoration of this city-dwelling priestess, you have led us closer to an ignoble death with each and every step. You, who care more for these weaklings than your own kin, talk to me of honor? I Challenge you for leadership!" The capital C was clear in his voice.

Roland, the only archer of the group, raised an arrow to his bow but did not draw back. He shouted, "Challenges are only permitted within the arena and overseen by the Elders. You know this is our way. You have no right to issue one while in hostile territory!"

"And yet I issue a Challenge nonetheless." Thom grinned, and gave Angus a little shake. "I believe that this makes me entitled to an exception, don't you think?

Tilly scoffed. "You challenge me? Like you challenged me this springtime past? And the autumn before that? Have you already lost count of how many of your scars are my handiwork?" She drew her blade and brandished it at him. "Have a care, Thom, for if there is to be a Challenge, the outcome is final. When I pierce your black heart this time there will be no magic to return your breath or pump your blood." She spit a gobbet of phlegm into the glen. "And we will leave your corpse for the vermin, unmourned and unremembered."

"Thom can't fight you while he holds Angus hostage," Roland whispered. "As soon as steps aside I can fill that treacherous bastard with arrows."

Tilly kept her eyes on Thom as she weighed the options. Under ordinary circumstances doing so would be a stain upon her honor. However, as Thom himself had pointed out these were no ordinary circumstances. Further, this could have a serious impact upon their mission. If Thom won, her friends could be deserted, left to face the remainder of the journey and their meeting with Magnus on their own. If she defeated Thom, she herself could be gravely injured, and Allison's magic could only do so much. Cailin, standing nearby, urged her, "Do it."

Thom noticed the exchange and released his grip on Angus to wag a finger at them. "Oh, no no no. We'll have none of that. This is to be a *true* Challenge, with no interference." He swept his gaze across the others of the People arrayed along the edge of the glen. "See how quickly she was to give in to the dishonor of striking me down before we even locked blades?" He argued. "She does not deserve to lead."

"Then we are at an impasse," Allison called out. "Release the hostage, you are at our mercy. Kill the hostage, you are still at our mercy. Put down your dagger and give yourself up. There is no conclusion to this that works in your favor."

"Do you really believe that the rest of us would follow you after this?" Roland chimed in. "I've always thought you were a little cracked, but this is just too much. Your time with our people is at an end." There was a murmur of agreement from the others, including all those who had stayed with Thom at the farmhouse.

"Shut your hole, you coward," Thom barked back. "You fight with a coward's weapon and speak with a coward's tongue. Once I've dispensed with the captain, I'll see to you next." To Allison he added, "As for giving myself up, Lady, I think not." He whistled and several dozen men emerged from the trees behind him. They were clad in identical chain-and-mail armor and wore tabards emblazoned with the same rising-sun sigil as Hummelton's occupiers. "How about you throw down your weapons and give yourselves up to us?"

CHAPTER 13

The two groups eyed each other across the glen. Tilly, Allison and Jimmy stood just inside the trees, with the others arranged loosely in the brush behind them. The People were lightly armored and wielded swords or axes in one hand and round wooden shields in the other. Behind Thom, on the far side of the clearing, stood a company of armored soldiers in tight formation, shoulder to shoulder. Four men standing near a plumed officer held longbows at the ready.

"This is idiocy," growled Tilly. Even if any of my people aren't cut down by arrow fire as they run, they will just be skewered on spearpoints."

"Then we walk away?" Asked Jimmy. "There is no dishonor in wise tactics."

She shook her head firmly. "Not with Angus still in their hands." She turned to survey her followers, and when her eyes fell on Ashley she said, "We will speak more of this later," before taking a step forward. "I accept your Challenge for leadership," she announced to the silence. "And this time I'll kill you for good."

"You can't do that," hissed Allison, tugging her back by her shoulder. "If you win those archers will turn you into a pincushion."

"What would you have me do?" Tilly spat, her eyes fierce. "Leave Angus to have his throat slit like a hog and his body left as offal?" Her voice softened. "No, Lady. My honor led me to your journey. It now leads me to this fight, even if it means my journey ends prematurely." Cait stepped forward and handed Tilly a shield, which she secured tightly to her arm. Tilly gave her sword a few experimental slashes to limber up before stepping toward the center of the clearing.

"Please wait!" Allison begged. "Just for a second." The other woman turned to meet her gaze. Allison crossed the short distance between them and placed a hand upon Tilly's shoulder. "May the blessings of the Goddess protect you," Allison murmured, then lightly placed her lips on her friend's forehead. With the kiss came a burst of power that ran down the entire length of Tilly's body. The fatigue from weeks on the was road was washed away, leaving her with both a renewed sense of purpose and inner fire.

"Thank you, Lady," she murmured, eyes moist, then turned back to their enemies.

Thom leered evilly at Tilly as she approached. He pushed Angus to the ground and sheathed his dagger before drawing his sword, a longer version of Tilly's. While not as large as Jimmy's massive weapon, Thom's blade was still designed to be swung with two hands. It was the type of weapon that beat an enemy into submission rather than slipping through their defenses. When Tilly had crossed about a third of the distance one of the bowmen raised his weapon, but Thom waved him down. "I have been looking forward to this a lonnng time," he said, stepping forward to meet his nemesis.

"Ever since the last time I beat you, I bet." Tilly scoffed. And then they met.

To the friends it felt almost like a repeat of the Challenge between the Warlord and his older brother they had witnessed outside Providence City. It was, once again, a battle between the smaller, more agile, embracer of change and the larger, stronger, keeper of the old ways. It was also a battle to the death, with no quarter asked or given.

From the very beginning, Thom's strategy was clear: over and over he took mighty two-handed swings, trying to knock Tilly off her balance. Whatever strategy Tilly had planned quickly devolved into a desperate series of dodges, blocks, and parries. Each powerful blow of his blade against the shield on her arm sent shock waves into her shoulder and her left hand soon went numb from the repeated strikes. From time to time Tilly's sword slashed out at exposed flesh, but more often than not Thom dodged aside, so she did her best to take his attacks and hoped that he would tire before her shield split.

On the far side of the clearing the soldiers watched impassively, though the one who had taken control of Angus occasionally gave the bound man a shake. The archers held their bows at their sides, but all had arrows nocked. The People, in contrast, hooted and hollered and shouted words of encouragement to their captain. Roland had spoken true: they had no appetite to follow Thom even if he were to win the Challenge. "Well if we're going by cheering sections, Tilly's got him beat," Allison commented. "It is eerie how quiet they are."

"That is simply because they care not who wins," TJ replied coldly.

"No?" Allison was surprised.

"Nope," answered Jimmy for the wizard. "Whoever comes out on top, they have orders to kill all of us."

"Wait, what?"

TJ picked the thread back up. "Isn't it obvious? If you learned there was a plot to kill you, would you let the assassins go on their merry way after some ridiculous battle of honor? I wouldn't. If Thom loses, we carry on with the plan to kill the general. If Thom wins, well, would you trust someone who sold out his clansmen out over a fit of jealousy? That man is a liability, for sure."

Some of the People in hearing distance shifted their feet uncomfortably, as if TJ's assessment made more sense than they preferred. The wizard turned and smiled at the group behind him. "Not that you have anything to worry about." Allison caught a glimpse of TJ the boy peeking through Galphalon the wizard's eyes. "Those soldiers, my friends, are in what we refer to as 'fireball formation.' They don't appear to have encountered a wizard of my caliber before." He peered at where they stood at near-attention and chuckled. "Or any wizard, possibly. No matter, they will not have the opportunity to repeat this mistake, I can assure you. Were it not for your friend Angus, I would have already settled the matter. He *is* your friend, correct?"

Cailin, already visibly anxious about Jimmy's and TJ's assessment of the soldier's orders, visibly paled. Suspicious of magic by nature, there was something about the casual manner with which TJ suggested using his power to kill two dozen men at once that made the young man's skin crawl. Had TJ noticed Cailin's reaction he may have found it amusing, but as soon as he had finished speaking he'd ceased paying the others any attention.

Behind them, Chuck spoke for the first time since they arrived at the glen. "Unless I misheard dear Galphalon here, I believe that was my cue." He bobbed his head and tipped an imaginary cap, saying, "If you would excuse me, ladies, gentlemen." He squeezed between a pair of horses standing shoulder to shoulder, ducked under another, and slipped back into the woods.

The fight in the clearing continued to rage. As Tilly had hoped, Thom's swings became weaker over time. Unaware of Allison's blessing, he had poured too much energy and bile into his initial onslaught and his strength had already begun to flag. Tilly took a sudden opportunity to slash out with her own sword and drove him several steps backwards. It didn't take him entirely off the offensive, but she saw not being in constant retreat as a minor victory. Thom, his initial rage wearing off, recognized her strategy and adjusted his own tactics accordingly. Instead of simply hammering at her shield, he mixed in a slice or thrust from time to time.

Finally, one of his changeups caught Tilly by surprise. She had raised her shield to deflect what she thought was another of his powerful downward strikes, but at the last moment he twisted his grip and swung the blade low, toward her legs. She managed to partially deflect the slash with her own sword, but still his blade bit deep into her left thigh, drawing a splash of blood and a gasp of pain. He pressed his advantage, slashing twice more in rapid succession, and though she blocked both the difficulty with which she staggered out of range brought a wide grin to his face. Using the momentary break in the action to gloat, Thom spread his arms wide and spun in a slow circle, looking first at the soldiers he had brought, then at his former comrades, and finally back at Tilly. She scowled at him even as she limped backwards, blood oozing out of her leg wound. He approached her slowly, sneering. "What's the matter, *Captain?* Not feeling like your old self? Not feeling like the self you were before you gave up our people's ways and prostrated yourself before these weak city dwellers?"

"You've gone mad, haven't you?" Tilly gasped at him. "Are you really so hell bent on proving that you're better than me that you're willing to throw away your life?" She shook her head as she continued, "If you think any of our people would follow you after this, you are sadly mistaken. All you will be left with are those city folk you so despise." She pointed at the soldiers arrayed on the far side of the clearing. "You are nothing but their lapdog. When the Warlord learns of what you have done today, you will be exiled forever."

Thom's brow furrowed and he looked past her to where his former comrades stood watching. Some met his look with stone-faced glares, others disdain and hatred. Sudden realization washed over his face and he turned to look at the soldiers behind him only to see the officer command the four bowmen to fire their weapons. Two arrows landed squarely in Thom's chest, and another hit Tilly in the shoulder, spinning her sideways and toppling her to the ground. One arrow shot wide, its archer toppled by an arrow launched from elsewhere in the clearing.

Before the first man's death registered with the other soldiers, a second arrow sped from the woods. Another archer dropped and confusion spread within the soldier's ranks. As if by some silent signal, everyone sprang into motion. The two remaining archers scanned the forest frantically to find who had killed their fellows.

The spearmen raised their shields protectively, and the officer began shouting. "Kill the prisoner and form up ranks," he ordered as he drew his sword. Hearing no response to his command, he looked for the man charged with guarding Angus only to find him lying face down in the dirt, a pool of blood slowly expanding out from him. Nearby, a second soldier hunched over, trying to reach the dagger lodged between his ribs, and just beyond him Chuck and Angus dodged between trees as they raced for their lives.

Across the glen, Jimmy leapt forward when the first arrows flew, whooping and swinging his enormous sword high. The People followed his lead, shouting battle cries of their own, spurring TJ to roll his eyes. "Didn't they hear what I said?" He grumbled. He leaned toward Allison and continued, almost conspiratorially, "This is what you get when you work with people like him. I have been dealing with this from Jameson for years, and he never seems to learn." He uttered a phrase that slithered eel-like through Allison's ears while tracing a series of geometric figures with one hand. A pea-sized ball of fire formed in front of him, and when he made a flicking motion with his other hand it sped away over his charging allies and toward the spearmen. The flame grew as it crossed the distance, and by the time it reached the soldiers it had grown to the size of a soccer ball. The fireball crashed into the ground at the spearmen's feet and exploded, sending a dozen or more of them flying in every direction. Those who were not immediately incapacitated were still stunned by its concussive blast, giving the People time to cover the remaining distance. The two sides began to hack, slash, and stab at each other.

"For instance," TJ continued as if nothing had happened, "Jameson should have long ago learned that the easiest way to deal with this sort of problem is with fire, preferably from far away. And yet, at the first sign of trouble, what does he do? He tears off like a dog trailing a hare through the woods, unconcerned for the finer parts of strategy, or even his own well-being. Seriously," he asked in disgust, "what am I supposed to do with someone like that?"

Allison nodded understandingly, all too aware of the how surreal it was to listen to her friend's complaints at the same time that swords clanged against each other mere yards away. She cut him off, "I totally understand what you're saying, and I agree that we really ought to have a talk with Jimmy about this some time." TJ's eyes grew excited at the thought of having an ally in his oft-recurring argument with the berserker. "However, she continued quickly before he could reply, "how about we table this for a while, perhaps until after all the excitement has settled down? Great!" She concluded for the both of them. "Now, if you would excuse me, I have some work to do of my own." She patted him on the shoulder and ran forward into the clearing gripping her mace loosely. Tilly lay injured and bleeding, and she needed Allison's attention far more than the wizard did.

When Allison reached Tilly's body, she found her friend bleeding heavily, though her eyes were open and alert. The injured woman gave Allison a wan smile and said, "Well that didn't go so bad, did it?" Her eyes then rolled back in her head and she lost consciousness.

As she had done many times before, Allison reached into herself to draw forth her healing power. Once again, the divine magic coursed up from the earth itself to flow through her and do her bidding. It felt different this time, however. In the past, it was as if a flood of charged water used her body as a conduit to reach the wounded person. This time, beyond the simple thrum of power racing into and out of her, she felt a presence. There was a Being creating and guiding and delivering that power, and the Being was both beneficent and terrifying. Allison knew without a doubt that this Being loved her deeply, and had consciously, specifically chosen to imbue her with the power to bless, heal, and perhaps someday even raise the dead. It was this same Being who granted her the power to smite her foes, by direct the earth's power in a violent outburst. And that same Being could, if it chose to, remorselessly tear her to pieces without even the slightest effort.

So that was what it meant to be the servant of a god.

As the realization of her communion washed over Allison, uncontrollable shakes took hold of her. From time to time since coming into this world, memories of her time spent as neophyte, then initiate, then ordained priestess flitted through her head. Those memories hinted at growing closer to her patron, but they had been but images and vague recollections that she, the fifteen year-old, knew were figments of her imagination. But this ... this was an unfiltered experience of the divine for which she'd had no preparation, and she felt as if the very cells of her body might explode in both joy and terror. After what seemed like an eternity of this power racing through her to her friend, each moment of which felt like it could be her last alive, the power faded and her mind cleared. She was surprised to discover that the eternity had lasted the briefest hint of a second. Tilly's wounds had healed, and the arrow had been expelled from her shoulder, but Jimmy and the others had just reached the line of soldiers, and TJ was still visibly rolling his eyes at the entire situation. As the enormity of what she had just experienced became clear, her fragile mind decided that it had had enough for one day, and promptly turned itself off, leaving her to slump into unconsciousness atop Tilly's resting body.

CHAPTER 14

Allison awoke to find herself resting on a thick bed of pine needles, a rolled up cloak beneath her head and another draped over her like a blanket. She sat up, sending the world spinning as it had the morning after her first experience drinking too much ale. She buried her face in her hands and tried to rub away both the dizziness and the damp hair stuck to her cheeks, letting out a slight groan as she did.

"Hey there, sleepyhead!" Jimmy smiled down at her from where he sat against a nearby tree. Across his legs lay his enormous sword, a buffing cloth draped over top. The sword was magical and never actually needed to be sharpened, but he still enjoyed the time cradling it in his hands and polishing it to a bright shine. On more than one occasion she had found him grinning at his own reflection in the enchanted blade.

"I take it we won?" Allison asked, looking around the glen. "How long was I out?"

"Yes, we won. Your being alive and able to ask such a silly question at all should have clued you in. We took our share of knocks, to be sure, but we carried the day. As for your second question," he looked upwards, attempting to gauge through the trees how far the sun had traveled. "Not long, maybe a half hour at most. After it was all over, we found the pair of you snoozing away in a pile, smiles on both of your faces. We saw the beating Tilly took, and even with your healing her body needs a lot of rest so we let her be. She's still out, and is probably going to be for a while yet. You, on the other hand, didn't appear hurt, but nothing we could do could bring you 'round." He smiled at her mischievously. "I even dumped some water on your face, but you just kept on snoring. It was pretty impressive."

"Well that explains my wet hair, I guess." She took another look around the clearing and noticed that the group had set up camp despite the early hour. They had erected several small tents, and atop a cook fire sat a kettle giving off both steam and a glorious smell. Her stomach growled and she rubbed at it absently. Near one of the tents sat several of the People with bandages across heads or on limbs, and Cait's left arm was in a sling. Allison scrambled toward them anxiously, but her legs betrayed her and she collapsed back to the ground after only a couple steps. Jimmy was there in an instant.

"Easy there, kid," he cooed. "They'll be okay without your help for a little longer." He looked her up and down and added, "Whatever happened to you, it's definitely taken a toll. Sit and rest."

Allison pointed at the makeshift clinic. "They're hurt and I can help them." She flashed an annoyed look at her friend. "Why didn't you try harder to wake me up?"

He shook his head. "I already told you, we tried pretty hard. And waking you up and earlier wouldn't have made any difference." He nodded toward the injured. "We got those folks all bound up well enough, and you can finish the job when you are feeling up to it. As to the others," he sighed. "Well, they went pretty quick. You wouldn't have had the chance to fix them up anyway." Allison surveyed the camp one more time, only then realizing that the group was smaller than before. She searched Jimmy's face and the way he wouldn't meet her eyes made her think that if she hadn't been unconscious, maybe more would still be alive. After a moment he continued, "So for now, just relax, have a drink, and take some deep breaths. We're going to be here until evening at the earliest, so there is no rush to get up on your feet."

Despite his encouragement to stay seated, she struggled to her feet, letting the disorientation wash over her as a form of penance. "No, I'm okay." She waved his arm off and stood on wobbly legs, then staggered over to the makeshift hospital where she was greeted by optimistic faces. A quick scan of the injured told her which of them were in most serious need of aid, and she began there. First in line was Afner, who had a deep gash across his shoulder. Despite his calm exterior, she knew he must be in serious pain, and without magical healing he would almost certainly be dead within a day. Next was a woman who had taken a spear to one leg. She tried to stand to greet Allison but Allison waved the woman down and set to work. Next came Cait and her broken arm, which was haphazardly held together with a splint. And so on.

With each use of her power Allison felt that same communion with the divine. Her mind tried to shut itself down again and again, but she fought through the fatigue. While her character may have been raised in a temple, she herself had missed the opportunity to acclimate to the experience. She was determined to rectify that issue. Having already failed more than one of those she was there to protect, she refused to let it happen again. Each time she used her power the rush became a little easier to take, though it never completely abated. How could a mortal ever get used to channeling the power of a god, after all?

When the healing was done, Allison staggered back to where Tilly lay to check on her friend. Her insight told her that the woman was uninjured but still needed rest. Her own body told her that she needed to rest too, and she dropped back to the ground in exhaustion. After several quiet seconds she asked aloud, "So what did I miss?"

"Well," Chucks voice startled her and she opened her eyes to find that he was standing directly over to her. He blushed, "Sorry 'bout that. Habit, I guess. Anyway, Stu managed to show up at just the right time. He's the reason Tilly only took that one arrow, and the one who kept the other archers occupied long enough to keep them from killing anyone else. Those four alone could have taken out half of us during the charge, so it was a lucky thing."

"No it wasn't," TJ called out from nearby. "I told you all I had it under control."

Chuck made a sour face at their friend and continued, "Well anyway, once Jimmy and company got to the other side, things got a little dicey. You already saw to the wounded, and we lost three others in the fighting, including poor Ashley." He shook his head sadly. "I don't think anyone knew that she and Angus were a thing, and Thom promised to let him go if she led us to his little trap. Once the fighting broke out and she saw that I had gotten Angus free, she just went crazy. I saw her face when Thom stepped out of the woods, and I've never seen guilt like that. If you ask me, she'd made her mind up the moment she agreed to lead us here." He paused a second, then continued. "Anyway, we got the better end of the deal by a long shot in large part thanks to Galphalon. Every one of those soldiers fought to the very end. I don't know if it from was devotion to their cause or terror at the thought of failing Magnus that drove them, but not a one asked for quarter. Thirty to three isn't a bad trade, all things considered." His expression made clear he didn't really believe it himself.

Chuck continued, "I was able to get Angus away before the explosion, though he's pretty shook up, as you might guess, so you'll want to pay him a visit in his tent. Poor guy didn't know that Thom had finally lost it—guess those little outbursts had been pretty common. When he came across Thom in the woods, they just got to chatting, and that traitor knocked him out and dragged him to the enemy camp to be interrogated. The poor guy didn't actually know any more than Thom already told them, but they didn't believe him and gave him a heck of a beating. And, of course, he knows what happened to Ashley. That's not helping either." Chuck shrugged. "Anyway, that's the short version of what happened."

"What about Stu?" Allison asked. "How come he disappeared on us?"

"He was alternately running for his life and stalking his prey." Stu had crept up on her other side, and his response made her jump.

"Would you guys stop *doing that*?" she demanded. Her friend was unperturbed.

"I was fortunate enough to not encounter Thom out there, but I ran into trouble of my own. Their scouts were roving further than we expected. One I took unawares with an arrow. Another, however, was far stealthier than I was expecting, and only the greatest of luck kept me alive. I bent forward to examine a footprint in the loam just as he released an arrow toward me. I then spent the better part of a day and night dodging to and fro, with him hot on my trail. Each time I thought I had lost him and stopped to catch my breath another arrow came from somewhere out of view." Stu smiled grimly. "I've never run so far and so fast, and no matter where I ran or where I hid, he was there."

"How did you get away?" Allison asked, rapt at Stu's story.

"Another stroke of dumb luck. A thick patch of clouds crossed over the moon just as I came across a small cliff face. The entire area was shrouded in darkness, and I saw a cave leading from of the rock. With nothing left to try, I dodged into the opening. As it happened, an unusually large porcupine decided to use the same hiding place for the night and we each scared the heck out of each other. The poor creature fled along the cliff, making quite the clamor as it did." He scratched his dark curly hair. "I guess my shadow thought that the porcupine was me, and I saw him step out of the trees to creep after it. Not one to look a gift quill pig in the mouth, I put a pair of arrows in his back. He may have been the better woodsman, but there's no one better than me with a bow. And speaking of luck, it was a good thing that he didn't have a partner cause the clouds moved aside just as I stepped out from the cave. I would've been an easy target, for sure." He shrugged. "In any case, I gave his body a quick search and ran back to find you. I got here just as things started to get dicey, and, well, you know the rest," he concluded with a slight nod and fell silent. He seemed almost embarrassed to have said so much at once.

Allison smiled at her friend. "Well we're grateful that you made it back to us alive, and even more so for your great timing. Who knows how things would have turned out if you hadn't taken care of those archers." TJ gave a conspicuous cough, but no one paid him any mind.

"So ..." Chuck said with a wink, "did he have any good loot?"

"Yes he did," Stu said. "Even lying on the ground with my arrows in his back I had trouble focusing on his body. I think it was because of this." He opened his pack and withdrew a hooded cloak that looked no different than those the others wore. It was dyed a muted green and the clasp at the neck was in the shape of a leaf. Chuck looked at it and yawned widely.

"I said good loot," Chuck scoffed.

"Oh, you know better than that," snorted TJ, suddenly very interested in the conversation. "Let me look at that." He held his hand out impatiently, and after only the briefest hesitation Stu handed the garment over. TJ immediately inspected it from top to bottom, spending a particularly long time on the silver clasp. After about a minute of silent examination he grunted and placed it back in Stu's outstretched arm. When he saw the others staring at him he asked in irritation, "What?" After a moment he seemed to realize what they wanted and he added, "Oh. It's magical, of course, though everyone should have realized that already." He addressed Stu. "You said you shot him in the back, right? Hold up the cloak." Stu did so and TJ pointed to the dangling cloth. "No holes in the fabric. It mended itself between the time our archer friend extracted the arrows from the corpse and now. It would have been interesting to watch it happen, but no matter about that," he waved his hand in dismissal. "The cloak's aura is far too strong for a simple self-repairing cloak. Obviously it enhances to one's ability to hide. That's why Stu had so much trouble." Chuck's eyes lit up as his mind raced through the opportunities such an item opened up.

"No, little one," TJ said condescendingly. "I doubt it would work within a city. Its color alone suggests that it is to be used outdoors, though I guess that could just be an adaptation to its current environment." He rubbed his chin thoughtfully. "I feel like I am missing something else about it—its aura really is quite strong. I will have to conduct some experiments in my laboratory when I get the chance. In the meantime, we should leave it at 'finders keepers,' as I believe I have heard you say on occasion?"

"Hah!" Chuck laughed, and raised a hand in a mock toast. "I hate it when my own words are used against me. Especially," he added, "in a court of law!" The others chuckled at his self-deprecating joke, enjoying the easy camaraderie they had shared over the years in their adventures. A good sense of humor had smoothed over many arguments in the past, and was very much a part of what had made them such a successful adventuring party. A comfortable silence settled over them as they retreated into their own thoughts.

Tilly suddenly sat bolt upright and looked around in a panic. "What did I miss?"

CHAPTER 15

"It is tonight or not at all," Tilly asserted. "They know we're here, and if neither their scouts nor soldiers are back by first light tomorrow, they'll know we're still here. At that point, they'll either leave outright or they'll increase their defenses, making a strike impossible."

"If it were up to me," Jimmy offered, "I'd still have extra sentries posted overnight just in case. Like you said, they know we're here, and they'd be foolish to assume they're safe just because they sent out a group of spearmen with Thom. For all they knew, he was leading their soldiers into a trap of his own." He took a deep breath. "Not that I am suggesting we call it off. We're never going to get a better chance to learn about where Magnus is hiding. This is the only thread we have."

"Agreed," Allison said. "I wish we still had the element of surprise, but I also wish I were a princess in a castle. Neither are true." She looked to Stu and Angus, who sat together on the other side of the makeshift war council. "Did either of you see what we're going to run into?"

He shook his head and sighed, "No. I ran into Thom before I got that close and the next thing I knew he had whacked me on the head. I had a sack over my head the entire time I was in their camp, but it didn't sound like they had a lot of men with them. Just say the word and I'll get back out there, and I am not going to get tricked this time." His initial grief over Ashley's death had turned to rage, and he was clearly itching for a fight.

Stu nodded his head as the other spoke. "I got close, but not enough to provide any intel. If Angus and I leave now we can get there and back before you break camp. Hopefully they won't have anyone else with enchanted cloaks waiting for us."

Allison decided. "Then go," she said. "If we start off in an hour or two, we will get there when they're least alert. We leave at full dark, whether you're back or not." The two men nodded and jogged off together without looking back. Allison waved her arm vaguely in the direction of where they had buried their dead. "I feel like we just had this conversation and it didn't turn out so well. I pray this time goes better."

Tilly patted her on the shoulder. "It will."

The group prepared for the assault as they waited for their scouts to return. Swords were sharpened and bindings on armor were double checked. Some of the People offered prayers to ask for aid in the coming fight or beg for mercy in the afterlife. By the time darkness fell, all were ready to move. Neither Stu nor Angus had returned, but they knew where the camp was and set out, hopeful that one or both of them would find them along the way. Not long into their march the two came jogging toward them from different directions. The pair had split up just outside the camp to assess the perimeter's defenses in half the time. While Stu, with the aid of his new magical cloak, passed undetected, Angus encountered a roving sentry who had to be silenced before he could raise the alarm.

Tilly called a halt to let their scouts catch their breath and tell them what they'd seen. Stu spoke first. "It's just as we hoped—the camp is small, though large enough that I'm happy we aren't taking them on in daylight. The squad they sent with Thom looks like it was a sizable chunk of their strength, so they are weakened. Most of the sentries are posted within the camp's firelight, so we ought to be able to get pretty close without alerting them. Even so, as Angus can attest, we'll still need to be watchful as we approach. From the brief look I got, there is no observable pattern, so we will just have to trust the gods to smile upon us." Angus nodded as Stu gave his report, occasionally offering a grunt in agreement.

When Stu fell silent, Angus picked up the thread. "I counted a half dozen tents large enough to house ten or more soldiers and their gear. There was also a large pavilion where the general and whomever he is meeting are sure to be spending the night. Two guards are posted outside the headquarters, but they, along with the perimeter sentries, are the only ones awake."

"In other words, just like we found at Hummelton," Jimmy summarized, smiling. "And that worked out just fine."

"It is," murmured Allison. "And that worries me. They know we're out here and have had no word from the soldiers they sent with Thom.. Why are they so lax in their security? Could they really be so foolhardy?"

"Brash and pompous, more like." Afner snorted. "Just like these city folk armies to underestimate our strength. We will crush them like we always crush them. It is our way." Some of the others nodded agreement at his statement.

"And yet," Allison cautioned, "now we are the brash ones, assuming that these soldiers will be easy pickings. That may or may not be true." She looked around at the assembled fighters. "There is no margin for error. There are no reinforcements. If we lose here, Magnus wins, and his rule will spread over the continent."

"You said at the beginning of this journey that you would take what opportunities you could," Tilly argued. "Isn't this the sort of opportunity that the fates have granted you in the past?"

Allison looked at her friends, as the fight's outcome had particular importance for them. Each, in turn, nodded their willingness to proceed. She sighed, doubt chewing at her. "So be it." She smoothed out a patch of dirt, then broke a twig off a nearby bush and handed it to Stu. "Show us what you saw."

CHAPTER 16

The plan was simple: they would approach the camp silently, neutralizing any sentries they encountered. TJ's magic would provide artillery, and with luck they would meet as little resistance as they hoped. The general could not be allowed to escape, and three of the People, including Roland, were assigned to watch for him. Allison said a prayer to the goddess, just as she did over Tilly earlier in the day. She knew that while it was less potent when shared among the group than when focused on an individual, it was still better than nothing. If even a single additional ally lived through the night, it was worth it.

Stu, Tilly, and TJ would lead one group of fighters, who would attack from the far side of the camp. Jimmy, Allison, and Chuck would lead another, with the People shared between the two groups. Jimmy suggested that Chuck, though not a woodsman, was the best choice to creep ahead of his group to disable the sentries. Allison noticed a shadow briefly cross Chuck's face—as if he were weighing some deep decision—before he shrugged and retrieved a small wooden case from an inner flap of his cloak. As the others watched curiously, he deftly assembled a blow gun from its component pieces, then carefully dipped three darts into a small vial. He raised a hand to forestall any questions and said, "If we survive all this, maybe I'll tell you my story. But for now, just let me work." One of the darts went into the blow gun, and he wrapped the other two in a thin strip of leather, which he tucked into his sleeve. After carefully returning the vial to the case and packing the case away, he nodded his head. "Okay, I'm ready." He slipped ahead and the two groups set off.

Drifting clouds mottled the evening sky, and the moon cast wan light upon the ground. The clouds, together with a soft breeze, cast everything into motion so that it was difficult to tell if a patch of gray and black was a sentry, a nighttime predator looking for dinner, or simply a small tree swaying from side to side. Allison knew that this worked both ways and that their enemies would be just as hampered by the darkness, but that was cold comfort. Every member of their group that they would lose that night—and they would surely lose more than one—was irreplaceable, whereas the army had thousands upon thousands of reinforcements.

A twig snapped nearby and everyone froze. Jimmy winced and shrugged apologetically, as it was he who had misplaced his foot. The others shot him dirty looks before continuing forward. The camp's perimeter was close, and they would encounter sentries soon. As if on cue, Allison stepped over a log to discover a soldier's prone body, a bow laying not far away. The body had pushed tightly against the wood to make him blend into its outline. Her innate healer's intuition drew her eyes to his neck, from which jutted a small dart. She gave a slight shudder at how quickly Chuck's venom had worked on this man; he probably hadn't even known he had been attacked before he died.

Across the camp, Stu ranged ahead of his group, leaving Tilly and TJ with the others. His new cloak enveloped him, adding its enchantment to his already prodigious stealth. It was no wonder that he'd had such trouble spotting his pursuer—magic like this made it almost too easy to do his job. Almost. Of course, a magic cloak couldn't substitute for eyes that could spot the thin, ankle-height tripwire that he currently studied. He tied a pair of white ribbons around it several feet apart so the others would know to step over it. He wished that Chuck were with him, as there was a difference between spotting a tripwire and knowing how to disable it. If one of his comrades didn't see the ribbons, or stumbled at the wrong time, it would still activate.

The wire disappeared into the darkness in both directions, and he slowly followed it to the left. It passed through some low shrubs and was knotted to a tree several yards further along. The tree, as far as he could tell, was completely ordinary, neither rigged to fall nor fitted with bells to ring an alarm. It was, he hoped, simply a tie off point, with the other side being the active one. He quickly made his way back to the ribbons, and, seeing TJ and the others, waved at them and pointed to the wire. Tilly immediately nodded her understanding, and signaled a halt. Stu then followed the wire in the other direction, where again he found it again tied to a tree. He shook his head in disbelief. It was absurd to think it was there just to trip any attackers charging through the darkness, but he could identify no other purpose for it. Again, he wished for Chuck's expertise.

He signaled to Tilly that he was moving forward and stepped carefully over the wire. The entire area was suddenly bathed in blinding light, and behind him, TJ and the others threw up their hands to block the glow light. The cloak that had until that moment kept him hidden from view blazed ferociously, casting him in stark relief against the dark night. To his friends' horror, Stu continued to creep forward at a crouch, apparently unaware of how he stood out. A half dozen bowmen with arrows drawn stepped out from a nearby tent, and before TJ could finish an incantation, six arrows streaked toward Stu. He collapsed to the ground, and his cloak's light was extinguished, returning the area to darkness.

TJ completed his spell, and a ball of fire streaked toward the bowmen, all of whom were drawing a second arrow. The ball exploded in their midst, killing or incapacitating them all. All pretext of stealth forgotten, the men and women around him charged forward into the camp, battle cries on their tongues. Tilly led the charge, leaving TJ to stagger toward his friend, afraid yet certain of what he would find. As he ran he raised a wall of flame to shield Stu and himself from the fighting. The ranger's body lay still, his blank eyes staring upward. All six arrows had found their mark, no doubt piercing lungs and heart. A trembling fit came over the wizard, his vision turned blurry, and he felt a new channel to the primal forces of the universe open up to him. Looking up from Stu's corpse, he discovered a soldier making a beeline for him from the side of the wall. TJ extended a hand and raw power flowed from it into the charging man, who flashed brightly then collapsed. He dismissed the flaming wall as he stood, then slowly made his way toward the center of the camp, flinging energy at every enemy he saw.

The other group saw the flash of light and heard the shouts

of Tilly's charge. They all knew it was too soon, which meant something had gone wrong. Unable to communicate with the others, their only option was to charge ahead and hope for the best. Jimmy raced forward, his sword swinging wildly as he bellowed a northern battle cry. This was echoed by the others, who rushed forward in his wake. As Allison tightened her grip on her mace and let out her own yell, something tugged at her consciousness, causing her to stagger. She couldn't put her finger on what, but something terrible had happened. Something much worse than a broken twig or alerting a sentry to their presence. She shook her head to clear the fuzziness that had taken over and resumed her march.

Jimmy found the camp far more active than they'd expected, and braziers had sprung to life, bathing the entire area in bright light. He saw a large wall of fire and bodies scattered beside a flaming tent. Tilly swung her sword left and right as she led grim-faced fighters into the camp. There were already more enemies in view than there should have been, and fully armored soldiers continued to pour out of the tents. Had they known that this was what they would face, they never would have planned the attack, and he let out a curse at their overconfidence. *Of course,* the general wouldn't have let down his guard like that. Those kinds of officers rarely lived long enough to be promoted.

Jimmy zigged and zagged as he ran, dodging the first flight of arrows launched in his direction. Some of those arrows found other targets in his allies, but he charged onward. It was up to Allison to tend to the wounded. His long strides brought him to the line of archers just as they drew their second arrows, and with a mighty crosswise slash he slew two men outright, as well as destroying several other's bows. Behind the archers stood a line of spearmen readying to step forward with shields. Unprepared for Jimmy's quick advance, they scrambled to set spears but once again he swung his sword, knocking aside their weapons. He lowered his shoulder and bowled into them, then began hacking relentlessly. The others arrayed behind him quickly cut down the remaining archers and joined Jimmy in the scrum. From time to time lightning flashed, sending clumps of dirt flying and filling the air with the scent of ozone. Jimmy hoped it was TJ's doing.

Behind them, Allison saw the arrows strike her allies, and as goddess-driven instincts prioritized the injuries she moved from person to person, channeling only enough power to get the wounded back into the fray. The dizziness and sheer joy of her connection to the divine had become easier to take, but having fallen unconscious from its power once, she paced herself. She, too, needed to stay in the fight. None of the arrows had struck mortal wounds, and she gave a silent prayer of thanks. She had no way of knowing if her blessing had made a difference, but that didn't matter. She had a lot to be grateful for, regardless. She felt more than heard, *You're welcome, little one*, and energy coursed through her.

Chuck had scurried into the camp well before the chaos broke out, and he slipped from shadow to shadow as he made his way toward the general's pavilion. Soldiers ran to and fro as the multi-directional attack taxed their ability to respond effectively. He ducked into a nearby tent as a half dozen spearmen ran past and found an elderly hunch-backed man chanting quietly over a large red crystal that pulsed with light. Smoke drifted lazily from a nearby brazier, lending the air a sweet, musty tang. Small bolts of electricity darted from his hands to the crystal, each accompanied by a booming explosion outside the tent.

Chuck drew a stiletto from his boot and crept closer to the wizard. He'd only the barest instruction in the magical arts—only enough to avoid or disable enchanted traps—but it didn't take a prodigy to know that whatever magics were happening here were making lives difficult for his friends outside. While Jimmy loved to valiantly lead others into battle, knives in the dark was where Chuck excelled. And from his experience, his knife could affect a battle's outcome far more than Jimmy's charge.

Before Chuck could take more than single step the wizard's head jerked toward where he crouched. The old man's eyes were rheumy and unfocused, yet seemed to know exactly where to look. Instinctively, the rogue spread his arms innocently, though he knew there was little point.

The wizard smiled grotesquely, each tooth filed to a point, inscribed with mystical runes, or replaced outright with a gem. "Oh," he crooned, "what do we have here? A little mouse come to play with kitty?" His voice was raspy, devoid of emotion, as if a snake had learned to speak with just its tongue. Chuck tried to advance but found his feet motionless, firmly planted to the ground. The old man wiggled two fingers and Chuck's hand moved of its own accord, jabbing the stiletto into his thigh. He gasped, eliciting a chuckle from the wizard's misshapen mouth. "Yes, a very little mouse." Outside the tent the booming had ceased, though the clang of steel and the cries of those wounded continued to echo.

Chuck felt the full power of the wizard's attention bearing down on him, enveloping him in energy. This was no simple hedge wizard, Chuck realized, but one of the elders of the Arcanum itself.

"But what sort of game would little mousey care to play?"

The wizard's eyes squinted tight and Chuck felt his mind laid bare. One after another the memories flipped past. The streets. The training. The girl. The betrayal. Thoughts he had suppressed for years were exposed and he involuntarily cringed with each one. "Ahh," his tormentor said. "This one fears his past. Yet there is so much for him to be proud of," he crooned. Chuck's first theft. His first kill. His first contract. The girl. The betrayal. He felt as if he were a book and the wizard was tearing out pages to feed to the fire. He would soon be completely empty, everything that made him who he was charred to ash.

The image of another elderly wizard appeared, one free of the horrific visage sitting across the tent, and Chuck clung to it. He was firm but not unkind as he put the boy through his paces. Chuck knew that the old man could have snuffed him like a candle, though for some reason continued to let him live. He showed the boy things, wonderful, amazing things, things that he could have learned to do as well had he put his mind to it. But the boy lacked the patience for that sort of study. Or perhaps he just lacked the vision to see what his life would have become if he left the streets to train as an arcanist rather than a thief and assassin. Nonetheless, the wizard had done the best he could with the recalcitrant student. Determined to a pursue a life of crime the boy had focused on magical traps and other wards. Yet some of his other lessons stuck.

In particular, among the first skills he had gained was a mental preparation trick. More experienced wizards such as Galphalon could channel their magic at will whereas those newer to the art risked burning themselves out, both literally and figuratively. Young students were shown how to achieve an out-of-body experience from which they watched and guided themselves through more complicated and dangerous magics. As the old man in front of him continued to leaf through images of his past, Chuck centered himself and cast his psyche outward as he'd been instructed. In his mind's eye, he could see himself frozen in place, blood oozing from his wounds. The wizard continued to watch gleefully as pieces of Chuck's inner self burned, unaware of his captive's projection. Chuck carefully reached out from where he hovered and tried to move one of his fingers. Not only did the digit wiggle smoothly, the movement went unnoticed.

Chuck took a mental 'breath,' then in one fluid motion raised his empty hand to unsheathe a throwing knife from his other arm. The wizard squinted briefly, then his eyes opened wide in amazement at the astral image floating nearby. Chuck felt the page-tearing cease as the old man began to chant a different spell, but before it was complete Chuck had thrown the blade, which flew straight to the wizard's throat. He gasped the remaining syllables of his incantation, but the blade had severed his vocal chords and all he emitted was a vague hiss. His hold on Chuck dissolved, and the little man returned to his body. He leapt forward, yanking the stiletto from his own leg and plunging it into the wizard's heart.

It was as if time stood still. Everything quieted, from the sounds of steel on steel to the orders barked by officers to the shouts of fighting. The wizard locked eyes with Chuck while his withered body collapsed in on itself. Then, and as time rushed to catch up with itself, the old man exploded in a surge of raw power, sending both the tent and an unconscious Chuck flying.

As the wizard died, much of the camp disappeared into nothingness, including the general's pavilion, many of the other tents, and most of the soldiers running between them. Corpses that had had been struck down faded away, and a new clarity settled upon those who remained. Attackers facing six or seven soldiers found only one or two in front of them, or even none at all. TJ, eyes still burning with an angry fire, made quick work of those still standing, and soon the only sounds that remained were of the injured calling out to Allison for healing.

In less than fifteen minutes, all of the defenders and more than half of the attackers had been killed.

CHAPTER 17

"So this whole thing was one big trap?" Allison fumed. "How could we be so stupid?" She looked around the ransacked campsite, now far smaller than it had originally appeared. Flames still burned within the braziers, casting ominous, flickering shadows everywhere. Although they had left the solder's bodies where they fell, the survivors had carefully arranged their fallen allies in a row to one side of the camp. Burying them would have to wait until morning. For now, all they had the energy to do was commiserate over their losses and direct anger at Magnus.

Realizing that they had been tricked, that there was no meeting and no general and nothing but one of Magnus' minions making them dance had nearly broken the group's morale. Just as much as it pained the friends to have lost Stu, each of the People felt an equally keen loss at their own friends' and loved ones' deaths. Dying in battle was nothing new to the nomadic group, and was even glorified in song and ode, but their grief was intense nonetheless. Cailin, for instance, sat slumped next to his sister, his hands clasping hers. His were yet warm, hers had cooled.

"If it is any consolation," TJ offered, "not even I saw through the illusion, nor did I recognize that Stu's cloak was cursed. If I could be deceived, you should not expect anything more from yourself."

To Allison it sounded like her best friend had paid her a sideways compliment, reminding her of how much smarter he was than she. Even so, she found it surprisingly consoling, given the circumstances. It had been months since they lost Simon, and now that Stu was gone, the reality of their plight once again came into focus. This wasn't a game, they weren't just a bunch of characters, and despite the fact that luck had smiled on them again and again, they were all just one mistake away from death. She wiped an angry tear from her cheek and nodded her head.

"Thank you, I think. But that doesn't bring Stu back, or Olav or any of the others. And doesn't change the fact that we only fell into this trap because of the letters Chuck found in Hummelton. And we only we found those because Becka stumbled upon our camp and because Chuck can't keep himself from snooping around for valuables." The little man raised his hand in a mock salute. "Was this Magnus's plan from the very beginning, leading us by the nose from place to place?" She turned to Tilly. "For all we know, your joining us was part of his plan as well."

The other woman scowled back. "Do you think so little of us that you would accuse us of helping that monster? We mourn our dead as well, Lady."

Seeing an argument in the making, Jimmy interrupted. "Now

Tilly, that's not what she meant and you know it. Don't let your grief blind you to the fact that we are all friends here." He held her gaze until she nodded curtly before continuing, "More importantly, does any of that change what we do next? "Say that Magnus knows where we're going." He began to tick off a list with his fingers. "Say that he also has the ability to push us in whichever direction he chooses. Say even that he has already decided when and where to fight us. So what? Does that mean we just go back west and hide inside Providence City's, or go back north to our home, or even hire a ship and sail to Freeport? All any of that does is put off the inevitable."

"And given the mess that made me leave Freeport in the first place, the inevitable wouldn't be put off very far," Chuck muttered, only to be shushed by Jimmy.

"Magnus has set his eyes to the west and will capture Providence City when he marches in force. His armies will move north, south, across the sea, and sooner or later he will control everything. And then, when there is nowhere left to run and all our allies are dead or enslaved, then what will we do? Stand up to him?" he scoffed. "He'll crush us like bugs.

"Even worse," the northman stood and looked around the circle of survivors, and continued in a softer voice, "he could just leave us be. There we'll sit, drinking away the hours of our lives in some tavern without even the dignity of a death earned by fighting for something. However many more years we live, we'll be chained to the knowledge that we had the chance to do something, the chance to exact vengeance on the one who had caused us so much pain ... and the memory of having done nothing. The chance may be slim, but I would rather take that chance now and join Stu in the afterlife than to let it pass me by and die of old age, a dotard, honorless."

He drew his sword and thrust it into the hard earth, driving the blade more than a foot deep. "Who will take that chance with me?"

CHAPTER 18

Magnus laughed from atop his golden throne. He had hatched many plots during his rise to power, had woven many complex deceptions that left allies and foes alike grasping for understanding. As a youth, he had even pulled a chair out from under his brother, bruising both his sibling's backside and his pride. None of those successes filled with him as much satisfaction and joy as he now felt.

He had watched the entire situation unfold through the link between the enchanted mirror in his study and the crystal in the wizard's tent. The five, with their barbarian allies, had crept so carefully through the grass, unaware that they were being observed by Magnus and by the wizard Mystirius, his minion in the camp. Magnus shook his head as his former colleague's name rolled through his mind. *Mystirius.* Some took such silly, pompous, names, as if their power alone wasn't enough to cow the common man. Perhaps, in retrospect, the old man had been correct, since his power had clearly not been sufficient. Maybe if he had told the little assassin his name it would have helped. He chuckled.

Most delightful of all was seeing the woodsman fall into his trap. Magnus had spent many hours researching and testing the magics necessary to provide the dual-purpose cloak. Many magical items existed to improve the wearer's stealth, and he had, in fact, captured quite a few from rivals in his own rise to power, bestowing them on those of his followers he deemed worthiest. Further, creating light from raw magic was among the first skills students must master before attempting more difficult and dangerous abilities. But melding the two opposites together into an item that revealed one power but hid the other? No one had done such a thing before, nor perhaps even tried. Why would they, after all? It took a very special intellect—*his* intellect, to make a fine point of it—to see the possibilities of such an item.

It was almost too easy, in retrospect. The poor man didn't even know he was lit up like a harvest fire for all to see, and almost certainly died thinking that he was yet unseen. An archer felled by arrows, a sneak betrayed by his own stealth. Delicious.

He had figured that either the northman or the rogue would also die during the attack. Until the very last moment it looked as if Mystirius would be the end of the little man. That all four survived gave him great joy, for he so loved this little game. After all, had he truly wanted them all dead he could simply have assigned more soldiers to the task, or just done the job himself. No, he had not yet finished playing.

And the icing atop the cake? That fool Mystirius was out of his hair as well. While the man had professed fealty, Magnus knew his ambitions hadn't been quelled. Because the sad old wizard had failed to realize how completely he'd been beaten, he was inherently dangerous. Not dangerous to Magnus himself, of course, but dangerous to both his plans and his fun, and that made him a liability. Well, now he wasn't.

CHAPTER 19

The following morning they laid their dead to rest. Again, Allison was tasked with standing in for the People's mystics at the ceremony, and she handled it all well enough until it came time to bury Stu.

Months had passed and the friends had traveled many miles since doing the same for their friend Simon. At that point, they had only just discovered that their fantasy world had become real, and the overwhelming emotion they felt was shock. Shock that their fun weekend had become so much more; shock that one of their friends could be struck down so easily without knowing that he should, or even could, fight back. At that point, they were just a bunch of kids with no idea what to do.

Now, months later, emotions were different. After so much time together and so many battles fought, they felt like they had lost a part of themselves. While Stu had never been much of a conversationalist, becoming only more reserved as time passed, his presence was constant. Even in the cramped quarters of Providence City he had stayed by their side despite how much doing so pained him. The bonds they had forged made him far more than a high school friend, he had become one part of a whole.

The friends decided to dig him a grave rather than raise a cairn, and they took turns digging at the hard ground until the hole was deep enough to ensure his body would not be molested by scavengers looking for an easy meal. Chuck commented that they probably didn't need to dig it as deep as normal, since the soldiers' bodies would feed a pack of wolves for a week, but after a stern look from Jimmy he continued his turn with the shovel.

"I don't know if I can keep doing this," Allison murmured after she placed last shovel of dirt over the grave.

"We have to, Allie," Jimmy said softly, but firmly. "What else is there for us to do?"

Allison looked up at him, eyes red from crying. "I don't mean the quest, Jimmy." She gestured toward the mound of earth. "This. I can't keep burying my friends. Who's next? You? Chuck? TJ?" Her voice caught and tears returned to her eyes. "You asked me to be a healer, not an undertaker. I. Just. Can't."

He put his hand on her shoulder. "We don't always get a choice, do we? And anyway, didn't the Goddess choose you to be a healer? I thought you left home because you felt the calling. That's what you said at the time, at least."

Allison frowned. "Now's not the time for jokes, Jimmy," she blurted. "Maybe you still think it's all a game or something, but it stopped being fun ages ago." She threw she shovel down and stomped back to the camp.

Jimmy looked at his other friends, and while Chuck seemed almost embarrassed for her outburst, TJ offered, "These sorts of events often create crises of faith. She will either come out the other side stronger, or it will break her completely. Let's hope the Goddess sees her through."

In addition to being a friend Stu had been their scout, their source of game, and deadly with a bow. From a practical perspective, the "party" was now missing an integral part, calling into question their very ability to function effectively. Just as Allison had been assigned the role of healer out of need, Stu's ranger made the group stronger. They would miss his pathfinding, his tracking, and his ability to sense danger before any of the others. The road they now traveled was not only going to be lonelier, but also more dangerous.

After the briefest discussion, the four agreed to offer Roland Stu's enchanted bracers and bow. Chuck had discovered the bow in an abandoned dwarven fortress overrun by kobolds and the bracers had been gifts from the Bonecrushers, a tribe of goblins. Both were powerful works of magic, and, as the group's numbers dwindled, leaving them with Stu's grave was out of the question. The young man looked at the items with reverence bordering on awe.

"Are you sure that he would want me to have these, Lady?"

"Of course he would," she reassured him, patting him on the shoulder. "There is no one among us better suited to bearing these items than you." She paused before asking, "And what of you? Will your people accept your use of a weapon tainted by the arcane? I was under the impression that anything magical was frowned upon."

He shrugged. "Maybe they will, maybe they will not. As it is,

I'm already shamed for using a bow in the first place. If there is one thing that last night proved to us, it's that we face something far more formidable than a tribe of plains orcs or white creepers roving from the mountains. The way things used to be is not the way things must always be, especially if we are to actually have a future."

Tilly, sitting nearby, raised her water skin in salute. "Of those of us who came with you east, Thom was the only real follower of the old ways. And we saw where that brought him." She waved her arm at the destruction around them. "I, for one, welcome whatever will take us closer to the mad wizard behind all this, so that one of us can stab him through his black heart." She drank deeply from the skin, then stood and went to tend to her horse.

Roland grinned. "Well, there you have it." He strapped the bracers to his arms and his eyes widened as he felt their power infuse him. He nocked an arrow onto the enchanted bow, drew back the string, and aimed for a lone tree standing a hundred yards away. After waiting for a breeze to die down he released the string. The arrow sailed across the clearing and clipped the side of the tree.

Allison frowned. "Odd, Stu would have hit that. Could something have happened to the magic?"

Roland chuckled. "He was a far better archer than me to begin with. Yesterday I wouldn't have hit the tree at even half that distance. I think these are working just fine."

"Oh," she replied, reminded again of what they had lost in the fight.

No one cared to wear the magical cloak, even though the arrow holes had once again mended themselves, so they decided to burn it. Despite TJ's best efforts, he was unable to identify what had triggered the cloak's blinding radiance.

"For all I know there is not even a trigger at all." He explained. "Perhaps the wizard that Chuck killed did something to activate it, or there was a ward around the camp itself. The possibilities are endless, and even if I had access to the Collegium's lab I might not be able to solve this puzzle. The two magics are diametrically opposed, and theory says that they should not be able to inhabit the same artifact. Perhaps with more time and the advice of the masters I could figure this out, but here? Not a chance."

The garment at first resisted the flames, so they continued to feed the fire with whatever materials they could find around the campsite: furniture, fodder, even a tent, which ignited with a roar. As the blaze died down, the cloak's outline remained visible within the embers, and it wasn't until TJ added his own magical flame that the cloth finally unraveled and charred. Satisfied that the cause of so much suffering was destroyed, the group gathered up their horses and went on their way.

CHAPTER 20

Whether due to luck, their few numbers, or Angus being extra vigilant, the group encountered no other Arcanum forces for nearly two weeks. The evidence of armies on the march was everywhere, from deeply cut wheel ruts to an almost total absence of brush and small trees easily convertible to firewood. The biggest giveaways that large numbers of soldiers and camp followers had passed were the shallow latrines no one had bothered covering before moving on.

"The common soldier is a barbarian," TJ complained as he raised a scented handkerchief to his nose to block out the stench. "Have they no sense of decency? No self-respect?"

Jimmy barked a laugh at his friend's discomfort. "Decency and self-respect aren't as important to folks marching to war as it is to wizards in their towers, Galph. You've got to remember that these folks were expected to make a full day's march after breaking camp. It's far better to save your strength for battle than to use it all up filling holes."

"On the contrary," Allison countered as she swatted at the swarms of flies disturbed by their passing. "That's when decency and self-respect are most important. It keeps you from forgetting that you're human."

"If you say so, Allie," Jimmy replied with a smirk. "If you say so."

The massive mobilization made clear to the group that speed was of paramount importance. If they were to avert the oncoming war, they needed to confront Magnus as soon as they could. Whenever possible, the group stayed to paved roads, only taking to the cover of forest when Angus warned them of other travelers. They also encountered inhabited settlements on a near-daily basis. Rather than the villages abandoned by refugees fleeing west to Providence City, these farmsteads and hamlets remained essentially intact, with men and women going about their daily business as if there were not a massive army being unleashed upon nearby kingdoms. The only indication that the world was not at peace was the absence of young men working the fields. Rather, work was performed by women, children, and older men unfit to wield swords of spears. While the physical devastation of war had passed by these people, they had by no means escaped other, lingering, and more insidious damage. Even so, the friends couldn't count on being welcomed, and skirted them whenever possible.

Late fall was in full swing, and this included chilly nighttime temperatures. Even so, the denser population meant that they eventually had to give up fires at night, as there was no telling whether the locals were simply subjugated peoples or were truly loyal to Magnus. Their smaller numbers meant that turns at watch became more frequent and the combination of cold and lack of sleep began to wear on them all.

"What I wouldn't give for a nice hot stew right about now," groused Chuck one night as they sat in a loose cluster. The fresh provisions captured from the "general's camp" had been eaten with the first week leaving them only dried meat and hard cheese. It was nourishing, but hardly the sort of fare that one selected if given a choice. "Or a hot anything, to tell the truth." He gave a shiver as he looked at Jimmy, who leaned against a tree, his cloak loosely arrayed about him. "I don't know how you northerners do it. I feel like simply looking at you dressed like that is sucking the warmth out of me." He pulled his own cloak tighter around his body.

"I agree," TJ mused. "While I have on occasion enjoyed a nice soft cheese across fresh bread, or perhaps melted atop a roast, I confess that I would be satisfied to never eat such a product again." He held up a crumbly morsel of cheese and eyed it in the dim light. "It is odd how one's circumstance influences one's preferences. I never would have expected myself to hold such an anti-dairy opinion."

Angus had returned from making a circuit around their makeshift camp just in time to hear the pair's complaints. He planted his feet and placed his hands on his hips. "Yes, we all miss Stu, and I know that I am just a pale substitute. I'm sorry that I've not been able to bring you a deer or a couple rabbits for dinner each night the way he used to. I will try harder to please you in the future." He turned on his heel and strode off angrily, leaving the others to sit in confusion.

"What was that about?" Jimmy asked bemusedly. "How did he get from 'we would like to be warm' to 'no one appreciates me?'" He stood to follow, but Tilly called him back.

"Let him be. He not only mourns a friend but is tasked with replacing one we all know is irreplaceable. That Roland was the obvious choice to bear Stu's weapon and armor only makes the pressure grow. I think the worst thing now would be to try to convince him otherwise. He'll deal with this on his own terms."

"He better." Chuck snorted. "We need to know we can count on him. I don't need to remind you that we're having to dodge around armed parties on an almost daily basis. We can't run the risk of another knock-down drag out fight."

Allison shot the rogue a stern look and replied, "He will. I have a sense of these things." Although she replied to his comment, her words were for the entire group's benefit, and as usual had an immediate effect.

"Aye, Lady," Inga agreed. "Angus is a good man, and he'll come around for sure." The others in the small group nodded agreement, and Allison hoped that none noticed Chuck rolling his eyes at her "sense." He was, of course, right, even if he shouldn't have said it aloud. Their small group couldn't afford any distractions at this point in their quest. She hoped that calming words, bolstered by her enchanted ring, would continue to keep everyone focused and in good spirits.

"Let's get some rest," she added, effectively ending the conversation. "We should start moving early tomorrow. As the end draws near I feel a greater urgency to get this done." She rolled over on her bedroll, pulled her cloak more tightly around her shoulders, and took her own advice.

CHAPTER 21

"There," Angus pointed toward a small cluster of shanties built up against the wall surrounding the Arcanum, and the others squinted from where they lay nearby. The city's militia had been effective in eliminating most available cover on the field immediately adjacent to the city walls and they all felt dangerously exposed despite the darkness. The moon provided just enough light to make the hovels' broad outlines visible. From time to time the friends saw faint shadows pass from one to the other, but whether they were of residents returning home or desperate thieves stealing from the even more desperate there was no way to tell. For all they knew they were residents returning home after stealing from their neighbors. Such was the circle of life among those unable to find work and not fit for army duty.

They had immediately discarded entering through the gate along with the regular traffic as an option. Not only was it guarded by several dozen heavily armed soldiers, even a cursory glance indicated that there were no men of fighting age passing through the gate—the carts bringing produce and other goods to the city from outlying areas were almost entirely driven by women, children, and the elderly. While Allison and the other women could have masqueraded as farmers or herders, Jimmy's presence would raise questions. The guards gave most of the carts a thorough search, so there was no chance they could hide the northman's great bulk from prying eyes.

Instead, Angus had spent the last three nights scouting the city's great curtain wall while the others hid just inside the edge of nearby woods. Each evening he slipped out to search for a way in and, having finally found one that night, returned early. He'd hurriedly lead them around the perimeter to a spot on the far side of the city. "The city watch doesn't appear to like the populace setting up their shacks out here. Can't say that I blame them, since it's obviously something of a security risk." He winked. "Yesterday I saw them tear down a bunch of houses a couple hundred yards away. Today this new batch sprung up. As often as these people rebuild, they may as well be nomads like us."

"Are we going to encounter any trouble from the people living there?" Allison asked quietly. "These folks aren't our enemies. Given the way that they're forced to live, maybe they'd even be willing to help us."

"I wouldn't count on that," Chuck replied. "These are my sorts of people, and they'd turn us in just as soon as look at us. Regime change is risky and wouldn't make their lives any better for a while, anyway. The cold hard coin they could get from collecting bounties are on our heads will get them into real homes tomorrow. I've certainly done worse for less. And for all we know, the bounties could be large enough to set them up for life." Allison grunted but didn't argue the point.

"Well let's get on it." Jimmy pushed himself onto his knees. "The longer we're out here the more likely we are to get seen by someone. Chuck, you can get us over the wall?"

"So long as you're not expecting to stand on my shoulders, shouldn't be a problem." He tittered, but his mirth didn't spread to the rest of the group.

Angus led toward the center of the shanty at a trot, veering slightly to the right as a light suddenly flared to life within a doorway. In less than a minute the group had crossed the open field and found themselves within the protection of the makeshift buildings. Chuck briefly eyed the city's wall before scampering up, fingers and boots finding easy purchase within seams in the mortar. He briefly disappeared from view before tossing a rope down to the others. Knots spaced every foot or two made climbing easy duty for even Allison in her heavy armor and it wasn't long before the entire group was standing atop the rampart. From where they stood they could see the true measure of the Arcanum's size. Few buildings had but a single story, and many rose as high as five. Despite the late hour light shone from many windows, and the sounds of music drifted toward them on the breeze. There was no guessing the city's population, but not only was it far larger than Providence City, it reminded Allison of some of the larger towns in Western Massachusetts. "Hurry," Tilly hissed, refocusing them on the mission at hand. They hurried down the ladders leading to the ground, grimacing at each creak of wood.

Unlike the crowded patch of buildings outside, there was a thirty-foot buffer between the inside of the walls and the nearest structures. The ground had been paved with tightly fitted stones of marble that faintly glowed of their own accord—no doubt infused with some trace of magic. Lantern glow from a sentry post shone from around a corner a scant hundred yards away, so Chuck led the group straight into the darkened alley between two buildings. Though far cleaner than the refuse-strewn alleys of Providence City, there were still crates haphazardly stacked against the walls and the friends easily hid themselves from any prying eyes at either of the alley's ends.

"Sit tight," Chuck whispered, then winked at Angus. "You did good. I'll take it from here." He scampered up one of the stacks of crates onto the roof and disappeared from sight.

"Sit tight," Jimmy muttered, shifting his weight back and forth from in agitation. "That's easy enough for him to say. He doesn't have to worry about having enough room to swing his sword in here." He eyed the span between walls and shook his head. With a grin, Tilly offered him a dagger hilt first. He snorted and patted the one at his hip. "Nah, I'm good."

"He enjoys complaining," TJ said, "especially when he is nervous. He has been like that ever since we sat outside King Robert's audience hall, and probably even longer than that." He raised an eyebrow to Allison.

"Yeah," she chuckled. "You should have heard him back on the soccer field! It was pitiful to watch." Her smile faded almost immediately—although she expected references to their old world to yield blank looks from the People the brief look of puzzlement on her old friends' faces took her aback. TJ and Jimmy both nodded and smiled, but Allison knew from their blank eyes that they were just humoring her. "Oh, never mind," she said and lapsed into silence.

After what felt like an eternity but was, in truth, no longer than half an hour Chuck's small form descended from above. "There is a warehouse nearby, only a couple minutes' jog from here, where we can hide out until we get our bearings. It's stocked up with weapons and other supplies in case the city is sieged, which means we probably won't be disturbed. Unless, of course," he added mirthfully, "you saw any armies marching this way that I didn't notice?"

Allison eyed the eaves above them skeptically. "Are we all going up there? I could probably make the climb ... with a rope, at least. But I'm not jumping from rooftop to rooftop with my armor, quietly or otherwise. We'll have the entire Arcanum chasing us in no time." Several of the People nodded their agreement. None looked happy at the idea of being within the city walls at all, let alone being twenty or thirty feet from the ground.

"Fear not, M'Lady," Chuck replied with a flourish. "There is an easy enough path to get there, though we'll need to move fast, and you'll need to stay close. I saw patrols moving along some of the larger streets but didn't take time to map their routes. I'll scout ahead from the rooftops, but even so we may cross one of their paths. The quicker we move the better."

"Well let's get going then," said Jimmy. "I'm getting claustrophobic."

"Agreed." Chuck reached up to pat his big friend on the shoulder comfortingly. "Head out that way and take a right. It's three blocks south, two to the west, and then one more to the south. If I think you need to change routes, I'll let you know. Cross the street here while we know there's no one watching. It'll be easier for you to keep me in view from the opposite side, anyway. " With that, the small man shinnied back up the crates and led them to the far mouth of the alley. "Let's go," he hissed from above and disappeared from view.

The street onto which they emerged was part of a lower-end commercial district. Among the businesses in evidence were butchers and bakers as well as lenders and at least one jeweler. Most prominent were taverns, however, and most appeared open for business despite the late hour. Music floated out from one or two, but by and large the only sounds were those of the patrons swearing, fighting, or calling for more ale. Jimmy's eyes fell upon the sign of one of such establishments, which featured stylized mountains with streams of yellow ale descending from snowcapped peaks. "Reminds me of home," he murmured, licking his lips but he moved on when Tilly smacked him on the back. "I'm moving, I'm moving!"

Chuck, across the street, darted ghostlike along the eaves. At each corner he sprang across the gap to the next roof, pausing only long enough to flash the others an all clear sign. He made them turn west one block earlier than originally planned when a guard patrol trooped past a little too close for comfort, but there were no complications, and in a matter of minutes they arrived at the warehouse's back entrance.

Chuck dropped to the ground lightly and said, "In we go," as he opened the door with a flourish. Once the others had all gone through he slipped in behind and closed and locked the door.

"So, now what?" Tilly asked. "We may not be standing around

in the streets anymore, but we're not much closer to our goal."

Chuck opened his mouth to reply but his words were cut off by a shrill voice. "You are closer than you think." The warehouse burst into light, an elderly woman robed in ornate red and black silk and leaning on a jewel-topped staff. Behind her a full company of glowering soldiers stood poised at the ready.

CHAPTER 22

Hands reached for weapons, and the woman called out, "Oh, I wouldn't do that if I were you." At the first sign of movement the soldiers raised their crossbows, more than one appearing eager to shoot. "I'm just here to talk, so there's no need for this to get messy," she continued, then tsked. "Though, if that's what you're looking for, we could wrap this all up right now and I can go back to bed. This is an ungodly hour, after all."

Blades slid back into sheaths, accompanied by a low murmuring and hostile glares at Chuck. The little man seemed unperturbed, though his eyes darted around the room looking for cover. After the briefest moment Allison stepped forward, arms spread wide.

"Blessings on you, friends." She gave a shallow bow and continued, "To what do we owe the pleasure of this meeting?" She beamed her friendliest smile and was gratified to see that the soldiers aiming their crossbows at her redirected their weapons to other targets.

"Oh, pipe down little girl," the wizard scoffed. "I am immune to your paltry little bauble and I don't overmuch care for your goddess or her blessings. You're not going to charm your way out of this." The force of her gaze made the younger woman unconsciously take a step back. "That's better. Let's get down to business. I have a proposition, and it not only gets you your revenge on our dear lord Magnus, but maybe even lets most of you keep your pathetic little lives." With a sly smile she repeated the word, "Maybe. As a show of good faith, my men will stand down. As I said, there's no need for this to get messy; if I kill you all now then none of us gets what we want." The soldiers flanking the wizard backed away and lowered their weapons. Seeing that none of the friends had relaxed, she rolled her eyes and shooed her men toward a large cart door. When they had all left the building she asked, "Satisfied?"

TJ scanned his companions' faces and finally nodded agreement. "So, who are you? What is this proposition of yours? And why, given that you command Arcanum troops, should we trust you?"

"Ahh," she purred, "right to business. A man of my own heart and, unless I am mistaken, of similar training. You studied at the Collegium, didn't you? I can sense that the earnestness of its masters rubbed off on you. How droll." She paused a moment to let her eyes run from one end of the party to the other, her gaze lingering on each of the four friends even as she ignored the People. "Well, for your first question you will have to accept disappointment. I know why you are here, and as much as I would love for you to kill Magnus, I wouldn't even wager money on it, let alone my life. Were he to leave any of you alive, my name can't be dancing across your lips if you don't know it. And for that matter, this is of course not my true appearance." The wizard tapped a finger against her mouth in thought for a few seconds before continuing, "But if you must, you can call me the Mistress." Her mouth split into a grin.

"This is ridiculous," Tilly murmured to Jimmy. "We should silence her and get moving. I've had enough of wizards for a lifetime, Galphalon included."

"Oh, kitten," the Mistress said. "This discussion isn't for you and your rabble. The grownups are talking, and it would be better for everyone, yourself included, if you didn't say another word." She waved her hand and Tilly felt her mouth snap shut. "Now that's better, don't you think?" She said into the silence with a smile. "As for my proposition, it is simple, really. I can get you straight into Magnus' chambers without having to draw your swords once. What you do once you're there is your business, but I seem to recall the girl saying you didn't have a plan from this point forward. If," she cackled, "you ever had a plan to begin with."

"Get on with it, witch," Jimmy snarled.

The woman drew a rolled parchment from one of her sleeves and held it up. "I have brought you a map to the city that includes the location of a hidden entrance to the palace. It was designed as an escape route by some long-dead king who thought it was better to flee than to die fighting." She made a sour face. "It has been many years since a wizard of the Arcanum thought to flee, so it has fallen from most people's memory. I have come to give you this map to hasten your journey."

"And ... ?" TJ said.

"And nothing. It's as simple as that. You need to get into

Magnus' inner chambers, and I'm giving you a way to get there."

This set the group to chattering about whether the map was real and if they should take it. Tilly, with her magically sealed mouth, grunted and gesticulated wildly. TJ shot Jimmy a look, and he then hushed the noise with a loud "Shhh!" When quiet had fallen TJ eyed the other wizard and said, "That is oddly generous of you. Why are you doing this, and why should we trust you? How do we know that you are not leading us into a trap?"

The Mistress rolled her eyes and sighed audibly. "Really? I already told you that if I wanted to kill you, I would have, and you must admit that I could have done it instead of revealing myself just now. So, let's put aside the thought that I'm somehow leading you to your death. Beyond that, how can you trust me? Because, my dears, I want Magnus dead every bit as much as you do."

"You do?" Allison asked.

"Of course I do, you fool! We in the Arcanum are always looking to kill our rivals, and he is the greatest rival of them all. None of us, including myself, will ever grow our influence while he sits on the throne, moving us all like puppets. The only reason he hasn't killed me is because he either regards me as a tool or worse," she grimaced, "not a rival at all."

"This seems like quite a risk for you to take for just the chance to get ahead," TJ countered. "If he found out you were assisting us, he would kill you immediately. Those soldiers, for instance, could talk."

Her face momentarily clouded before she replied, "It is true. I have another reason all my own. Magnus sacrificed my lover for his inane amusement, and for that, he owes me a life. His life."

"I'm sorry for your loss," consoled Allison.

"SILENCE!" She shouted. "It was you who killed him! That little rat of yours hiding in the shadows did it!" She took a breath to settle herself. "I would take your lives instead, but as satisfying as that might be, it would gain me nothing. If you defeat him, I will have my revenge. If you do not defeat him, I will still have my revenge."

"Who?," stammered Chuck. "Do you mean the old wizard at the ambush?"

"His name was Mystirius, Worm, and if you say another word, I'll kill you, my revenge on Magnus be damned!"

Chuck paled, bobbed his head, and faded back into the darkness.

"Wait," interjected Jimmy. "You knew about the cloak and the ambush?"

Her tone softened as she answered him. "Oh, you sweet child. Of course I did, but for what it's worth I argued against it. Well, how he decided to do it, at least. The cloak was a brilliant idea, to be sure, but I told him not to play with the stupid illusions and just double the number of soldiers. But for whatever reason he didn't, and so here we are." She shrugged. "And now the question is whether you will accept my help or not."

"If we kill him, will we be free to go? Will you let us return west?" TJ followed up.

Venom crept back into her voice, "If I never see you again, I would count *that* a blessing." She leered at Allison.

"Then we welcome your aid." TJ bowed to her and stepped forward, his arm outstretched to take the map. The other wizard walked towards him as well, and they met in the center of the warehouse. She handed TJ the parchment with a flourish and a smile. He returned to the group and handed it to Chuck, who immediately unrolled it and began scanning it for details.

"She killed my sister." The friends' heads all turned at Cailin's low rumble. He stood, shaking with anger and staring daggers at the wizard. She looked on with a smile, her attention focused on the map, and she didn't notice Cailin's sword leave its sheath. His roar echoed through the warehouse as he charged forward in a frenzy.

Suddenly aware of her danger, she reached out a hand and launched a bolt of energy at him. The blast spun him around and slowed his charge but didn't drop him. As he crossed the remaining distance she released a second energy bolt, which sent him to his knees. She grinned mirthlessly as she looked at him. "The foolishness of youth," she sneered, and began a complicated gesture that would summon a more powerful attack. Before she could complete the motion Roland drew and released an arrow, which struck her in the stomach and sent her to her knees. She looked up from where she knelt and flung an energy bolt at the archer. This gave Cailin the opportunity to regain his feet, stagger the rest of the distance between them, and arc his sword cleanly through her neck.

There was a moment of silence punctuated only by Cailin's labored breathing and then the soldiers came pouring back in from where they waited. Crossbow bolts filled the air, and

Cailin went down in a heap, his body falling atop the dead wizard. Some bolts landed among others of the People, who looked around in confusion. Inga immediately fell, as did Angus. Some made to draw their swords, but Chuck yelled, "You stand, you die! Follow me!" He threw open the back door and charged into the night, uncaring who followed and who didn't.

CHAPTER 23

The sound of booted feet and the flash of lights gave them only the barest warning before the first lines of Arcanum soldiers charged into the square. Every third or fourth man bore a torch in one hand, casting the plaza into bright, flickering, light. Instinctively, TJ raised a wall of flame between his group and their attackers, halting the advance. Angry threats came from behind the wall and a soldier beat at it with his cloak. Roland targeted him with an arrow, and the other soldiers, having gotten the message, retreated to find a different route.

As the first platoon withdrew from the square a second and third charged forward from other directions. Again, TJ called on magic to fend them off, this time with exploding balls of fire. The attackers were prepared, and most took cover before the spheres had crossed the distance. By the time they detonated, fewer than half of the men were injured by the blast. Roland followed up the explosions with a pair of arrows, both of which struck soldiers creeping out of hiding. Once again the soldiers scurried backwards.

During the lull the friends ducked down a side street and took off at a run. The city had been built haphazardly, and not only did the street wind to and fro, but many smaller passages sprung off in different directions. The road reminded Allison of one of her family trips to Boston, and how the narrow streets and sharp curves made driving awful, if not downright impossible. If she'd not been fleeing for her life, she'd have found the idea of future generations driving these streets of amusing. As it was, she was simply grateful that the twists and turns made it that much harder for enemy archers to target them from behind.

The noise from the pursuit didn't draw any of the city's inhabitants to investigate. Most had long since discovered that when you lived within the capital of a nation ruled by power-mad wizards it was rarely wise to stick your nose into others' business. Ignorance was, in most cases, truly bliss. Those who didn't understand this truism died in one of the many periodic purges as the wizards stamped out conspiracies, both real and imagined.

The group rounded yet another corner and ran headlong into a guard patrol. Both sides drew swords and the clash of steel rang out in the night. The patrol's officer blew into his whistle frantically, and its sound was echoed by others in the distance. Roland put a stop to the sound with an arrow in the officer's chest and one soldiers returned fire. Roland dodged but the missile struck his left arm and he reflexively dropped his bow. Magic weapon or no, it was useless to a one-armed archer so he left it where it fell. Instead, he snapped the arrow shaft near where it emerged from his arm and drew his sword.

Jimmy and Tilly stood shoulder to shoulder, hacking their way through opponents. They were lucky that this had been mere city guardsmen who rarely dealt with more than a drunken brawl. The pair efficiently cut down one after another, while TJ supplemented their assault with blasts of magic. Roland moved to join them, but Allison pulled him back to heal his arm. "Leave that to them. We need you to deal with enemy archers." He nodded, and after the burst of magic expelled the arrowhead and sealed his arm, he sheathed his sword and retrieved the bow. No one had yet answered the whistle's summons so he took several more shots at the guards. One turned to flee, shouting for help as he ran, and Roland shot the young man in the back. It may not have been the honorable choice, but he couldn't risk him bringing reinforcements.

As the fight raged, Chuck scaled up the side of one of the nearby buildings—a tannery, according to the sign. Unlike its neighbors it was a two-story affair, housing the business on the ground level and the tanner's family above. From the building's flat roof, he was able to see several blocks in each direction. Torchlight rushed toward them along several nearby streets, and he called out, "You've got about a minute or two to get this wrapped up, guys. Backup will be here soon!"

At his shout both sides redoubled their efforts, the friends trying to fight free and the defenders trying to hold their line long enough for help to arrive. The little man vaulted off the roof to land behind guards. The men wore steel plate on both their chests and backs, so he threw several daggers into exposed hamstrings. Two went down immediately as their legs gave out from under them and Tilly's quick blade made quick work of them. The others, surprised by the sudden attack from behind, were distracted just long enough for Jimmy to slice his enchanted blade through their defenses and finish them off. Without taking time to catch their breaths, the friends took off again, racing away from the approaching soldiers.

At last they reached their goal, a cul-de-sac at the base of a hill where the map said the hidden escape tunnel lay. TJ illuminated the area with dim globes of light and the others began searching for seams, hidden catches, or anything else that might indicate a door. Years of neglect, along with lichen and moss, concealed any obvious signs, and the residents of this neighborhood had discarded trash and rubble in the area for years. They were searching for the proverbial needle in a haystack, only doing it in semi-darkness and under threat of being swarmed by scores of soldiers.

"I think I found something," Allison shouted, pointing at a part of the rock face. The others crowded around, and TJ drew all the lights to hover nearby. "There," she said, pointing at a spot about two feet off the ground. The brighter light revealed a square about a yard on a side, and Jimmy reached out to touch the square. Chuck sprang forward and slapped his hand away.

"Always just barging in, big oaf," Chuck muttered as he squinted at the seam. After several seconds he pointed. "See there? Those rocks up there are rigged to collapse on anyone trying to open this from the outside. Luckily," he indicated a hair-thin wire dangling nearby, "it looks like the mechanism managed to disable itself over the years. No surprise really, if it's as old as the Mistress said. Still, be careful. A good tug will drop all that on our heads."

"Good. Let's go." Tilly cast an eye backwards. "We don't have long before they catch up." She drew a dagger and slid it into one of the seams. Chuck gave a yelp of surprise and slapped her hand aside just as he had Jimmy's.

"Never settle for a single trap!" he exclaimed. "There may be only one, but you should always count on three!"

"That ... seems excessive," she replied nervously, looking over her shoulder again.

"And so is my age for a thief," he snapped. "Now let me work."

Sure enough, within minutes Chuck had found both a small vent for poison gas and a cleverly disguised magic sigil designed to explode. While he plugged the hole and looked for secondary gas release outlets TJ uttered a series of arcane syllables to disable the magical trap. As the pair worked several soldiers trotted into the cul-de-sac. "There they are!" one shouted and turned his lantern's beam on the group. Roland felled him with an arrow, but another soldier darted back out of view, shouting as he went.

The remainder charged forward and Tilly and Jimmy stepped forward to meet them, the sheer ferocity of the pair's attack pushing the soldiers backward. The respite was only short lived, and they quickly found themselves hard pressed. Once again Roland dropped his bow and drew his sword to stand side by side with the others. "How about one of those walls right about now, TJ?" Jimmy shouted as he dodged a slash, then gave his own sword a mighty swing.

TJ looked up from the sigil distractedly. "Hmm?" Seeing the combat directly in front of him, he let out a little, "Oh!" and said, "Alas, I no longer have the ability to raise such a barrier, not expecting such a demand when last preparing my spells. Until I have some time to quietly study, I am afraid that other magics will have to do." He cast a ball of fire towards the base of a nearby building. The structure immediately caught fire and portions of it toppled into the street, creating a flaming barricade. A small shoeless child in a nightgown led a pair of wizened crones from the conflagration. The three staggered into the plaza, where the child called out to the soldiers in melee with Tilly and Jimmy. When they didn't immediately turn to address the boy, something clicked in his mind and he let out a cry of dismay, leading the oldsters away.

"TJ, stop that!" cried Allison. "People are living in those houses!"

The wizard seemed briefly confused by her complaint, "We would like to continue living as well, would we not?"

"Yes, but those people are innocents. Blow up the bad guys instead!" She stepped forward and touched Jimmy's arm, channeling a little healing magic to close a gash on the cheek scored by a soldier's a lucky blow.

"That should do it," Chuck proclaimed, ignoring the commotion behind him, and slid a wafer-thin blade into the seam. With a soft click, the square popped outward several inches, allowing Chuck to give it a soft tug. The stone slid out the rest of the way and landed on the ground with a deep *thunk*. He peered into the gently upward-sloping tunnel and was dismayed to find that it did not widen noticeably. In addition to its slight incline, the tunnel bent to the right, so even with

TJ's conjured light he could see no further than twenty or thirty feet.

"Ok, folks, everyone in!" he shouted and darted into the hole. His small stature gave him a significant advantage, and he quickly shinnied up.

"How's it look?" Tilly grunted as she parried another swing.

"Small and dark," Allison replied curtly. "But there aren't any soldiers trying to kill us up there. TJ, get in." TJ sent several balls of energy into a soldier who had begun to circle around the friends. The man fell to the ground motionless, smoke wafting from his chest. TJ nodded in satisfaction and stepped toward the hole.

Just then a large company of soldiers came running up the street. The flaming detritus provided a considerable obstacle but did not block the entire street, and several soldiers picked their way past. TJ sent another ball of fire streaking towards them, scattering many of the attackers. The buildings on that side of the street remained standing, however, and soldiers continued to pour in.

"Go!" Allison said, shoving the wizard harder. He gave her a curt nod and threw himself into the tunnel, scrambling awkwardly upwards as fast as his robes would let him. As his legs disappeared into the dark she shouted, "C'mon you three. We have to get moving!"

In front of her, Jimmy's massive sword crashed down, over and over, like a jackhammer. To his left, Tilly darted out to slash at any who tried to get inside his defense between strokes. To his right, Roland did what he could to hold his own against a brute of a man with a scar across his face. The three had held their position against the first bunch of attackers, but as the second, larger wave of soldiers clambered through the flaming wreckage the plaza took on a crowded feel. The three swordsmen slowly gave ground, inch by inch, backing toward the wall. "Go, Allie!" Jimmy panted. "We'll be right behind you!"

Allison hesitated, wondering how they could get into the passage without being stabbed from behind, as well as whether Jimmy's bulk was too large for the passage at all. Her friend sensed her hesitation and spared her the briefest glance as he recovered from a swing. "Go!" he insisted. In his face Allison saw a mix of emotions: Her friend from high school peered out, fear obvious in his eyes; the one who had promised her brother that he would look after her, had arrived at the temple just in time to save the day, and was determined to keep his promise one more time; the northern berserker who had faced death dozens of times in his short life and who always emerged alive, if not unscathed. His was the face of a man who knew he wouldn't fit through the escape hatch but was determined to see the rest of his friends make it out alive.

"You heard him, Lady Allison!" Tilly gasped as she drew her sword out from her opponent's chest. The brief lull gave her a moment to catch her breath. "Just go! We'll be right behind you, I promise!" Allison leaned toward the opening and Tilly gave her a shove. She toppled inward and felt someone pushing her forward from behind by her boots. She squirmed against the pressure, but couldn't gain enough leverage to resist, and soon found her entire body inside. Allison looked backwards and saw Tilly's earnest face looking back at her adoringly. "Forgive me, Lady," she half-murmured, then her face disappeared from view. A moment later, a jumble of dirt and rocks slid past, blocking the exit completely. Tilly had manually triggered the landslide trap Chuck had pointed out to them. In no time at all, tons of rock and scree collapsed around the tunnel's entrance, assuring TJ, Allison, and Chuck a safe escape while at the same time condemning the other three to death.

Allison hardly had time to process her friends' sacrifice before she felt a shock roll through her body, followed by a sudden emptiness. Her elbows gave out and she collapsed to the ground as she realized that Roland was gone. The experience repeated itself moments later as her connection to Tilly was also severed. Tears filled her eyes as she braced herself for the inevitable conclusion to the fight just beyond her reach. Even so, she was entirely unprepared for when Jimmy finally fell. Images of her and Jimmy growing up in Massachusetts came unbidden to her mind. These were joined by other memories, ones of a small village in the frozen mountains and a boy named Jameson, not Jimmy. They intermingled as they flashed past her vision, blurring the two Allisons and the two Jimmys. As suddenly as they began, they stopped, and Allison let out a sob at the finality of her loss. Unwilling to let their sacrifice go for nothing, Allison pulled herself forward to catch up with her friends, determined to destroy once and for all the wizard who had brought her so much misery.

CHAPTER 24

"I have news, Great Lord." The steward—the latest in a long line of stewards—knelt before Magnus' throne. The man was old, far older than Magnus himself, and as wrinkled as he was hunched. In fact, even with his cane's support he looked to be in danger of tipping over at any moment. Despite his age his eyes were bright and his desire to serve was obvious. Magnus couldn't help but notice that the newest stewards had been far older than those earlier in his reign. Was it paternalism that led the elderly to volunteer for this duty? The job's average lifespan wasn't terribly long, after all, and their doing so allowed the youngsters to live longer. He smiled, amused that his minions thought he could be manipulated so easily. Perhaps it was time for another random purge. Those were always fun.

The servant, misinterpreting Magnus' smile, beamed back at him as he waited to continue his speech. The wizard raised an inquisitive eyebrow and cocked his head to the side. The steward took this as assent and rose to speak.

"Our commanders report that the insurgents have been dealt with. Several dozen of our soldiers perished, and a portion of the Shambles is in flame, all it was done as you commanded."

Magnus waved his hand dismissively. Soldiers were a cheap commodity and that district had burned and been rebuilt so often there hadn't been an accurate map of it in decades. In some ways such destruction was good for society, giving the little people something to focus on rather than the drudgery of the day to day. If you teach a man to build, and then burn down his city, he will have work for a lifetime. That wasn't really how that quote went, but Magnus liked that version better than the original.

He leaned forward in his throne. "What more can you tell me? Were they taken alive? If so, how many were caught?"

The oldster's face fell slightly at the questions. The wizard's orders hadn't indicated that he wanted prisoners, so the soldiers themselves were given no such direction. Knowing his answer would disappoint his master, the servant softly sighed, wondering if his tenure in this position would set a new record for briefness. "There were three left, oh Wisdom. A woman and two men, one a northerner. They fought to the bitter end, and none were captured." He took a quick breath before finishing in a rush, "Had we known you wanted them captured I have no doubt that your servants would have done so." He knew doing so was a risk, but perhaps the wizard would see reason this time. Perhaps.

To the steward's surprise, Magnus leaned forward and clapped his hands. "Oh, very good! I hate prisoners anyway. You have to feed them, well at least a little, and I already know anything they might divulge so torturing them for information is a waste of time. Please see that the soldiers involved are properly rewarded." The wizard leaned back in his throne and absently rubbed the newly grown beard on his chin. "A woman and two men, one a northerner. Interesting. So, I wonder who is left ..."

"Your Greatness?" The servant looked up at Magus confusedly. "Who is left?"

"It is of no consequence to you. You have done well and you may go. Please inform the guard that they may have a night of relaxation. The end of this long ordeal is nearly upon us, and that is cause for celebration."

The steward hobbled away from the throne and disappeared through the large, gilt doors. Magnus watched him leave, still playing with his beard. Yes, the end was nearly upon them.

CHAPTER 25

"TJ, can you bring that light up here?" Chuck called from the end of the tunnel, about twenty feet ahead of the other two. TJ gave a sigh of relief, as it seemed to the wizard that they had been crawling forever. To Allison, time had slowed to a stop, as the psychic effects of feeling Jimmy die replayed in her mind. Thinking back, she realized that she had felt the same thing when Stu was killed in the ambush. Not that knowing would have made a difference. There was nothing she could have done anyway, and it would only have distracted her from keeping the rest of their group alive.

The rest of their group alive. So much for that. Not even a month earlier, the five of them had been accompanied by twenty-one brave members of the People, all of whom joined them out of gratitude and obligation, completely unaware of what lay ahead. And now, only she, Chuck, and TJ remained. Allison remembered each of the fallen's faces, both newcomers and lifelong friends. She knew that to let herself feel guilty about each death was counterproductive; just because she was a healer didn't mean that she would always be able to keep everyone alive. At the time she hadn't even known Stu was injured at all, though even if she had, his injuries were so grave that she wouldn't have been able to save his life even had she been standing directly next to him. She shook her head to clear her thoughts and continued crawling.

As she approached TJ's robed rear end, she heard a click followed by a soft, "Aha!" In the dim light she could just make out the smile on Chuck's face as he looked back. "That was easy enough," he whispered with a wink. "Now everyone hold your breath and hope this doesn't lead into their barracks or something. TJ please douse the light."

The wizard dismissed the magical sphere and thrust the tunnel into darkness. Chuck slowly drew open a small square door, which moved smoothly on well-oiled hinges. A crescent of light shone through the crack, and Chuck peered beyond. After a moment he opened the door the rest of the way and slid out nimbly. "It's okay, come on out guys!" he called softly, and soon TJ and Allison had joined him in a small storeroom lit by a crude chandelier holding several magical globes akin to TJ's.

Chuck pulled the worn map from his shirt and unfolded it carefully, then lay it on the ground. "Based on the size of this room and how far we just climbed, there are only a couple different places we may be." He pointed at three spots on the parchment as he said, "Here, here, or here." He traced his finger to a spot near the other side of the map. "And here is the throne room, where with luck we'll find Magnus." He ran a hand through his tousled hair. "I still wish we had a better plan than just confronting him and hoping for the best, but I guess this will bring us closure, one way or another. You don't think we could just call it all off and sneak back west? Getting out is always a whole lot easier than getting in, that's for sure." At Allison's blank look he continued, "Okay, okay, fine. We'll do it your way." More quietly he added, "Whatever way that is."

The three poured over the map to find the best route across the palace. "What about this marking here?" TJ asked, pointing at the map. "Is that what I think it is?"

To Chuck and Allison, he appeared to indicate nothing in particular. "What marking?" They asked in unison.

"Right there, don't you see it?" TJ slid his finger back and forth across the map, only stopping when he noticed his friends' confused faces. He withdrew a small piece of charcoal from his spell components pouch and said, "Right here," as he drew on the paper. When he was done, there was a pair of parallel, dotted lines running the length of the palace. One end touched off of the throne room's walls. "Is that what I think it is?"

Chuck barked a laugh before covering his mouth with his hand. "Yes, my friend, that is exactly what it looks like. Now the trick is to find where that tunnel starts and then find our way into it. Give me a second." He stepped to the door leading out, retrieving a necklace from a pouch as he walked. He slipped the chain over his neck, then cracked the door open to peek. His normally light footfalls became completely silent as the enchanted medallion he had liberated from the kobold's lair took effect. After a moment he opened the door the rest of the way, slipped out, and shut it silently behind him.

TJ and Allison shrugged at each other, and while Allison

crept toward the door, her mace held loosely at her side, TJ dusted off a crate with the hem of his robe and sat down to wait. Several minutes later the door again opened, startling the pair. When Chuck darted in Allison lowered her mace and TJ pretended to swat at a fly as if to hide the fact that he very nearly set Chuck on fire. The little man made a sour face at each before slipping the medallion off his neck and back into its pouch. "I appreciate the two of you not killing me," he said sourly.

"What did you find?" Allison asked impatiently.

"We are pretty close to where that tunnel starts. I didn't go all the way to its room, but based on what I saw, if the map is accurate there is really only one place we can be. If we hurry, we can be there in just a minute or two."

"What about the guards?" TJ asked, standing up from the crate. "I have quite a bit of magic left at my disposal, but it is not unlimited."

"I didn't see any just now, but you never know with these things. We might run into trouble at some point." He patted one of the throwing knives strapped to his arms and contin-ued, "Hopefully I can take care of anything we find."

"Well let's get moving," said Allison. "Lead the way!"

Once again Chuck opened the door and peeked out, this time without the necklace so that he could give instructions. He slipped through the door and gestured the other two to follow him. Allison and TJ nodded and followed Chuck, closing the door behind them. As with the storeroom, the hall was made from closely mortared stone blocks easily weighing hundreds of pounds apiece. Sconces held more of the glowing orbs and a long, thin, woolen carpet ran the length of the floor. The hallway was otherwise empty of decoration, as if someone had begun the process then got distracted before finishing.

The three crept down the hall, passing several doors on either side, all but one were closed. Through the open one they saw a bed and dresser against the far wall, both bare. The walls, however, sported intricate tapestries, one of which featured a knight astride a horse, his spear piercing the neck of a small dragon. The room had its own fireplace as well, though only charred wood sat in it now. Whoever had lived in this room had been someone important, but they, along with all their belongings, were long gone.

They wound their way through a maze of corridors, trusting to Chuck's sense of direction. Though not the best at navigating by stars, within the confines of a city, he seemed to know unerringly where to go. Only once did they encounter another person, a scullery maid carrying a tray with a large stack of bowls piled precariously upon it as she rushed down a side hallway. She didn't break stride as she passed; so intent was she on her own mission that she didn't even see the three infiltrators. Chuck raised an eyebrow to Allison, and put a hand on one of his throwing blades. She shot him a disapproving look, at which he shrugged and motioned them forward.

At last they found the room the map showed as containing the entrance to one end of the tunnel. The three slipped inside then closed and bolted the door behind them. They found themselves in a small library, all four walls covered by shelves crammed with books of myriad shapes and sizes. There were also two free-standing shelves in the middle of the room, also stuffed near to bursting. In one corner two opulent leather chairs sat facing each other, a small table stood between them, and a circular area rug lay just in front.

TJ immediately approached one of the bookcases and ran his finger down the books' spines as he read each title. Chuck looked at Allison, who rolled her eyes. "We may have lost him for the time being. Here, help me with this, just in case." She crossed to where the chairs sat and took hold of one by the arm rest. Chuck picked up the other side and the two maneuvered the it to sit against door as a makeshift barricade. It wasn't much, but after the experience just outside the palace, Allison was loathe to give up even the few extra seconds such a barrier would afford them. Maybe if the reinforcements had arrived half a minute later their three friends would have escaped alive as well.

Once the door was blocked Chuck got right to work searching the room for the secret tunnel's entrance. Allison eyed the door warily, a feeling of *déjà vu* settling over her. "Is there anything I can do to help, Chuck?" She started rifling through shelves as well, pulling books out at random in the hope of finding a hidden release.

"Chuck?" Allison asked after several long seconds without a response. She looked over her shoulder to find him eying a large wooden trap door in the floor, the rug in front of the chairs rolled up and pushed to the side. "Oh," she said sheepishly, and crossed to stand at his side. "I guess you found it already."

"Yup," he said, though his voice lacked its usual lilt and he sounded distant. His forehead scrunched as he stood there, deep in thought. "The question is how to open it." He began to ramble absentmindedly. "Of course, the way to open it is to simply pull on the handle," he indicated a small clasp in the wood, "but that's probably not the smartest choice right now."

Recognizing that her friend needed time to think, Allison backed away and sat in the chair against the door. The seat gave her a perfect view of the entire room, including not only Chuck's work but also of TJ as he leafed through a book. She chuckled softly at the thought of her homework-averse friend being engrossed in some tome of esoteric knowledge. While TJ read Chuck climbed atop the other chair and fiddled with a block in the wall. Now that he had drawn her attention to it, she noted that it had a slightly different shade than the stones surrounding it. She shook her head in amazement at Chuck's attention to detail. As she watched, he inserted a tool into a small crack in the wall and wiggled it several times. He then hopped back down, leaving the tool stuck into the seam.

"Was that it?" Allison called over quietly, and Chuck spared her only the briefest look before replying.

"Gas. That was number two. And what have I always told you?"

"The best things in life are free?" Allison replied with a smirk.

Chuck stuck out a tongue in reply. "You wound me, Allie. You truly do."

"I know, I know, always look for trap number three."

"Yup. It's not always going to be there, but more than once when I was younger I didn't bother to look and only avoided death by the sheerest of luck. Now I assume there's three until I'm confident there aren't." He went back to poking and prodding, now focusing on the bookcases facing the hidden door.

Allison leaned back in the chair and prepared to wait. If the scullery maid had seen them and told one of the palace guards, they probably would have already arrived. Since no one had shown up yet, maybe that meant that they were safe. Her eyes closed briefly, then jerked open again sometime later at the sound of Chuck's whoop. She looked up, to see him next to the open trap door, red-faced in embarrassment. His hand covered his mouth as if he needed to force it to stop making noise. "I take it you found it?" she asked.

"Yup!" he exclaimed triumphantly. "Just like I told you. This one would have dropped the whole ceiling on us. Let's go."

Allison looked upwards doubtfully, then hopped off the to stand next to TJ, who hadn't moved at Chuck's announcement. The book in his hand wasn't in any language she had ever read, and she wasn't even sure that it was in the standard alphabet. "Come on, TJ. It's time to get moving. We're almost there." Her friend absently nodded acknowledgment as his finger traced along several more lines of text. Only after she gave one of his sleeves a tug did he finally close the book with a soft thump and turn to follow.

"Oh! You're talking to me," he murmured. "This book is absolutely fascinating. It is a treatise on how the movement of stars and planets affect the lives of us mortals. An interesting idea, to be sure, though not one without some complications."

"You mean, *astrology*?" Allison scoffed.

"Oh, yes, that is an excellent word for it. Very clever." He patted her on the head like a dog who had done an exceptionally good trick and went to stand near Chuck.

The three looked at each other anxiously as they stood around the hole in the floor. A well-constructed stone staircase disappeared into darkness. Finally, Allison spoke. "On the other side of this passage is the end of a quest we have been working on for months. We have lost many friends along the way, both old and new." She looked each of them in the eyes before continuing. "Let's not blow this chance. For all I know, neither of you still remember the way things used to be, but I, for one, really want to go home and get back to my old life." Her friends' blank faces did not give any hint as to what they remembered or didn't. She reached out to her friends, and when they stepped closer she lay a hand on each of their brow before murmuring a quiet prayer to her goddess. When the blessing was complete she nodded to them. "Okay, let's go."

TJ summoned a light and floated it into the passage below, bringing the bottom of the stairs into view only ten feet away. The tunnel narrowed as it descended until it became only wide enough for one person to pass at a time. "It is all right," TJ reassured them. "A smaller tunnel is easier to hide in a floor plan. To Allison it sounded as if he were only speaking it for his own benefit, the tension having broken even his stoic, scholarly mien.

Chuck rubbed his hands together in expectation and began to descend. After a moment Allison followed, only a few paces behind. When Chuck put his foot on the fifth step down, he jumped back in surprise, flailing his arms wildly. Allison leapt to catch him and hissed. "What's the matter?" Chuck's body had gone stiff, so she dragged him back up to the library, bowling a surprised TJ over as she did. She lay Chuck on the floor and quickly looked him over from head to toe. His breath was hollow, his pupils dilated and he had broken into a sweat. He feebly reached for her hand and when she took it turned to look up to her face. "Fourth trap," he cracked a smile. "Heh. Didn't see that one coming. I wonder if this was your goddess' subtle way of telling me I should have led an honest life."

"It's okay, Chuck," she murmured, and closed her eyes to focus. She opened herself fully to her goddess' power, letting it wash over her in a way that she had never previously allowed. She had lost Stu without even knowing he was gone, and Jimmy had sacrificed himself so that the others could escape. She wouldn't lose a third friend now. No matter what it took, she *would* keep Chuck firmly in this world, even if she burned herself up in doing so. The power continued to build within her, and when she felt that she couldn't possibly hold it back any longer, she let it pour out of her, into Chuck, in a single, wild, rush.

It bounced. Rather than the healing energy infusing Chuck's body, it crashed back into her. It was as if a barrier existed in the space between them that kept her power on one side and his dying, limp form on the other.

Again, Allison activated the healing rush, and a second time the barrier reflected the power back into her, making her entire body shake with goddess-driven power. TJ reached out a hand to her shoulder and Allison swatted it away, failing to notice that the blow was enough to send her friend staggering backwards into the nearby chair. She gritted her teeth and closed her eyes, trying one last desperate attempt to save her dying friend. Instead of passively letting the magic flow, she actively pushed at it, using all her will and her very psyche to drive it through.

It did not work.

"DAMNIT!" Allison screamed, heedless of who might hear. Her voice reverberated around the room and through its walls.

TJ looked on from where he lay sprawled across the chair. He crawled back to where their friend lay and pointed to the bottom of Chuck's right boot. "Here," he said. Allison looked through bleary eyes at a shiny glint protruding a half inch from its sole. She yanked the metal out, revealing it to be a two-inch spike. Although smeared with blood, the residue of what it had been coated with was still visible. Whatever the poison was, it had been designed not just to kill quickly, but to also block magical healing, almost as if it had been placed just for this moment.

She shook her head angrily as she stood up, then marched straight down the stairs. "Allison! Wait!" TJ cried. There may be more traps!" She didn't even acknowledge him as she disappeared into the hole below.

CHAPTER 26

Moments later one of the throne room's walls exploded outward in a burst of flame and Allison and TJ strode through. At the end of the passage, the pair had once again come upon a hidden door. Certain that the door was warded with one or more traps and without Chuck to search and disarm it, they didn't want to risk simply opening it. "The solution is simple," TJ offered. "Stand back."

As the smoke cleared they saw him: Magnus leaned over a table, a golden goblet by his hand. He appeared engrossed in something, though how he could have missed the noise and smoke from the friends' entrance was beyond either of their understanding. TJ immediately hurled a ball of energy across the room and when the magical sphere connected with the wizard it exploded in a violent burst of rainbow colors. The bright lights dazzled Allison and she threw up her hands to protect her face. Once the blaze had died and the spots on their eyes cleared, they found the table had become a smoking ruin and TJ's target had disappeared.

"It can't be that easy," Allison murmured, but TJ grunted.

"You underestimate my power, Allison"

She shot him a questioning look, but he ignored it. She noticed that her friend stood a little more erect, his shoulders further back than she remembered. His eyes, which had always been dark, no longer had irises at all, their whites offset by pitch black emptiness. The faintest scent of ozone hung about him, and she felt his aura causing the hair on her arms to stick straight out. Somehow entering the very seat of the Arcanum's power had fundamentally changed him.

The pair were startled by a scraping noise to their left and they turned to look. Again they saw Magnus with his back to them, only this time seated. His chair was polished mahogany with leather and gold fittings, a perfect match for table at which he sat. His golden goblet now rested on the table, and his finger traced its rim lazily. TJ once again summoned his magic and hurled another glowing orb at the dark wizard. The pair watched more closely this time and saw TJ's attack connect with Magnus before exploding. The chair, the table, and Magnus had all disappeared, along with a piece of the floor.

"That seemed equally easy." Allison commented dryly.

TJ smirked. "Passive aggression is quite unbecoming, Allison." He crossed the room to inspect the smoking hole in the floor and Allison followed several steps behind. "You and I both saw the spell land, and there is nothing left." He gestured to the hole and it was just as he said. Nothing was left; even the floor had simply disintegrated. TJ made several motions with his hand while mumbling a chant, then nodded his head in satisfaction. "Easy, perhaps, but successful."

Allison opened her mouth to reply, but was interrupted by the sound of a throat being cleared. Once again, Magnus had reappeared. This time he stood near an open window and gazed out over the dark city below. A soft breeze blew through the window, tussling his hair and creating eddies in his robes, and he hummed softly to himself. The friends exchanged bemused looks, trying to reconcile the conflicting sights: on one hand a smoking ruin where their foe had been seated, and on the other side that same foe enjoying an evening breeze.

TJ drew several reagents from his pouch and began a complex series of incantations and hand gestures. His chant continued for five or six seconds and Allison looked back and forth between her friend and the man they had come to kill. As he completed his spell TJ thrust his hands forward and a beam of pure, radiant light poured forth and struck Magnus in the back. The lance of light continued unabated for half a minute, and while TJ's forehead began to wrinkle from exhaustion, the attack had no obvious effect on his target. It was as if the other wizard didn't even know he was being attacked. The exertion etched in TJ's face, however, made it clear to Allison that her friend was casting some pretty potent magic.

Slowly, Magnus turned to face the pair. The light pulsed over him, washing out his features and silhouetting his profile. For the first time since the pair had entered his throne room Magnus spoke.

"Oh children. Is this how you greet me after all we have been through?" He clicked his tongue and took a step toward them, not making any effort to step out of TJ's energy beam. "Put that away so we can talk like civilized people."

In response, TJ uttered several additional words and the beam changed colors, going from hot white to red, then blue, then back to red. With each color change the stress on TJ's face became more intense, and by the time the colors had finished changing his hands had begun to shake.

"TJ," Allison warned. "It's not working."

From across the room Magnus mimicked her, "TJ, it's not working! It's not working!"

TJ gritted his teeth and pushed harder. A thin trickle of blood dripped from his nose and Allison placed a hand on his arm. "Stop, TJ. You're killing yourself. Let's see what he has to say."

"SILENCE, PRIESTESS!" TJ commanded. "Do you not know who I am? I am Galphalon, commander of the arcane, slayer of the great wyrm Axram, and master of the fifth circle. This fell creature will cower before my power and beg for mercy. And perhaps I may even grant it." His eyes burned red and Allison retreated several paces from her friend, both awed and horrified at this sudden, final conclusion to his transformation from her geeky friend to wizard supreme.

Magnus appeared equally cowed. The wizard had fallen to his knees, his arms outstretched in supplication. The slightest hint of a smile quirked up one side of TJ's mouth, giving his face a look of deep satisfaction. His otherworldly eyes briefly left his target to lock on Allison's. "But then again," he murmured, "perhaps I will not." Once more TJ's beam intensified until Magnus' entire body was aflame. Sparks and sunbursts cascaded out in every direction.

Despite the fireworks, Magnus returned to his feet and dropped his arms to his side. Allison's eyes widened and she reflexively tightened her grip on her mace. TJ, however, hardly noticed, so enraptured he was by the magic flowing through his blood, a look of pure ecstasy plastered across his face. The other wizard walked slowly toward the pair, and it was only after Magnus had crossed half the distance did TJ realize something was amiss.

"No," he murmured, and redoubled his efforts. The heat from TJ's blast was so intense that Allison took several steps backwards to keep her own face and hands from being burned. Yet Magnus continued closer, step by slow, methodical, step. The flames around him had coalesced into a bright nimbus, and he smiled cruelly through the haze.

"Galphalon," Magnus began. "'Commander of the arcane.' 'Slayer of the great wyrm Axram.' 'Master of the fifth circle.' Did you expect any of those titles would impress me? Or even more laughably, cow me? You are but a child, a mewling infant toying with powers that you couldn't begin to understand, let alone call yours to control. You think that summoning flame makes you a wizard? I summoned more powerful flame than this when still at my mother's knee. You build shields of force to hide behind, but I build entire cities. You increase one friend's speed for a few minutes, but I manipulate the time stream in its entirety." With each word of his final sentence he reappeared at a different place in the room, finally returning to the center of TJ's energy beam at the word entirety.

He resumed his approach. "Poor children, did you think that you could walk into my palace and defeat me in a magical duel? Have you no idea of who I am or what I had to accomplish to become sole master of the Arcanum? I defeated dozens of wizards far more powerful than you, some in mage battles that leveled entire towns with their fury. And you, 'master of the fifth circle,' believed that you had any chance of defeating me?" He scoffed. "Perhaps I should visit your Collegium and teach your masters a lesson in what true power is."

Through this all Magnus's tirade, TJ continued to add power to his attack until his skin began to smoke, filling the chamber with the smell of brimstone. "I ... will ... destroy you!" he shouted, and charged Magnus, fire pouring not only from his hands but his eyes and mouth as well, and Allison had to shield her eyes from its brilliance. Magnus also continued forward, and the two wizards met in an explosion that sent Allison sliding backwards across the floor to collapse in a heap against the far wall.

When her head finally cleared and the blots of color disappeared from her vision she found the room in chaos, shattered furniture pushed against the walls just as she had been. In the middle of the room stood Magnus, apparently untouched by the magical cataclysm. Her eyes focused on his smiling face. A face she had seen before.

"You?"

CHAPTER 27

Before her, resplendent in his jeweled robes, stood the friendly, bearded face of the man she had thought was King Robert of Livonia. He waved a hand lazily and the destroyed furniture reassembled itself and slid back into its prior configuration. He made a second gesture upholstered in leather, as well as a small table, slid toward where he stood. Upon the table sat a crystal decanter of blood red liquid and a set of goblets.

"Yes, me." He flashed jazz hands and shouted, "Surprise! Bet you didn't see that one coming, did you? Come, have a seat, Lady Allison." He gestured to one chair and sat in the other, then filled the two goblets from the decanter. "They say that you shouldn't use real crystal anymore because of lead poisoning, but heavy metal is the least of my worries." He grinned and played an air guitar.

Although Allison had stood up, she hadn't approached the chairs, a mixture of surprise and betrayal upon her face. Not knowing whether to ask questions or burst into a tirade, she remained silent, slack-jawed.

"Oh, come on Allison. Don't be shy." He snapped his fingers and she slowly slid across the floor until she was standing in front of the other chair. Magnus gestured for her to sit and her body obliged despite herself. The chair was as comfortable as it looked, but she refused to enjoy it out of pure spite. They stared at each other for several minutes, she glowering, he smiling. At last, when it became clear to her that he wasn't going to speak first she asked, "But why?" It was the obvious, only, question.

"Ahh," he replied. "Right to the point! Very good. There are in fact several whys, so let's take them in turn. First: Why is Good King Robert an evil overlord?" He gave a mock shiver as he asked it. "That has the most obvious answer if you were to think about it. Let me be honest with you. Being a king is pretty great, actually. I doubt I had to tell you that, but there it is. Now, the only thing better than being the king of a small kingdom is being the king of a larger kingdom. And the only thing better than *that* is being king of *all* the kingdoms. I think I was doing a pretty good job of it, so why not expand? After all, that's what kings have always done.

"Now as it happens, my magical abilities manifested early, and my parents, goddess rest their souls, began my training when I was but three years old. You may not know this, but arcane magic is very much like a language. Just like children can pick up languages far more easily than adults, I took to spell casting like a duck takes to water." He gave a little chortle and nodded to where the floor was scorched from the explosion that took TJ's life. "Our dear Galphalon was so proud of his accomplishments, but I was a master of the fifth circle by the time I was twelve. So, long story short, when I felt ready, I came east to test myself against the other wizards here in the Arcanum. Sometimes I won. Other times I lost. All the times I learned, became craftier, and gained power.

"When my parents died I returned to Livonia to take the crown. I always knew I would have to, but I sincerely hoped - for both my parents' sake and my own, it would be when I was much older. Despite my initial disappointment it turned out to be a blessing. Splitting time between there and here slowed my magical growth, but I learned how much I enjoyed being a king, and that kept me motivated. It took longer than I expected to get to the top of the pyramid here, and I had to make concessions to some of my rivals, but now I here I am." He gestured toward the throne at the far end of the room. Speaking of which, thank you for disposing of Mystirius who you met at the general's camp, as well as his wife." He used air quotes around "general's camp." "He was quite the thorn in my side and I'm tickled pink that they're gone."

Allison listened to his story stony-faced. She didn't actually care about what drove him to power, but it was obvious that he had been looking forward to this talk and she knew he'd get to the more important answers soon enough. In the meanwhile, she was happy not to have to speak; she wasn't sure if she would be able to control her temper if she opened her mouth again.

"So anyway," Magnus continued, "the answer to why take over the world is because I both wanted to and was able to. Isn't that what has always driven Mankind to new heights? Why climb the mountain? Because it is there."

He drank deeply from his goblet and smacked his lips as he set it back down. "This really is quite good. Are you sure you don't want any?" Allison shook her head minutely and he added, "That's okay, your loss.

"Now a second, more immediate question: why did I send my realm's greatest heroes on a quest to defeat myself? Well, I have a few reasons for that. First," he held up a finger, "you are heroes, after all, and have made quite a career of rescuing damsels, defeating evil creatures, and generally standing up for what is good in the world. I didn't want you poking around and getting in my way back home. Livonia, you see, has changed somewhat since you left. Good King Robert has become a little less good. Wars are expensive and the western lands are wealthy. Much of that wealth has made its way to my coffers here in Estervary, much to my subjects' chagrin. That is exactly the sort of thing that heroes like you poke your noses into.

"Second,"—he held up another finger—"and this is related to the first, I knew that I would eventually have to deal with you, and if it happened before I was ready it was possible that you could have stopped me. That oaf Crackrock was to keep you busy until I could visit his dungeons and convince you to join me. You were always good, loyal minions when you worked for King Robert, and Magnus could use trusty servants too. Worst case, the ogre would kill you, since that's much of what ogres do. Alas, he bungled it both ways. Not only did I not get to speak with you, but he let you kill him and escape, no doubt after bragging about how well he and evil me worked together. Once he spilled the beans I knew you weren't joining me, so I just hoped you'd get killed somewhere along the journey. It is, after all," he winked, "a long and perilous trip."

"And last," he said, raising a third finger and grinning widely, "it was just a whole lot of fun to watch. I mean that was what you came looking for, wasn't it Allie? You and your friends, off on a wild adventure of killing creatures and taking their treasures? That is, as I said, exactly what heroes do! I, for one, had an absolute ball watching it play out, and I hope that the adventure turned out to be everything you expected it to be. I really hope you had fun too."

Allison, upon hearing this last, snapped. "Fun? You think this was all fun and games to us? My friends died out there, one just now in my arms. Have you ever experienced that? Watching a friend die in front of you, knowing you should be able to save them, but something," eye eyes narrowed, "or some*one* stops you? You planned it that way. You killed Chuck just as much as you killed TJ here in this room. And Stu, just like poor Simon, had no idea he was about to die. You set a trap and knew he would wear that cloak and it would get him killed. All my friends are dead, and it's because of you.

"And I've killed people too! I took this mace and bashed in a man's head." She stood up and shook it at him, though he remained placidly in his seat, smiling contentedly. "And do you know why? Because he was about to kill one of my friends. Maybe that's just another day in the office for you, but I'm fifteen. FIFTEEN. I've lost count of the number of people that I've killed and seen killed. And it's all because you thought it would be *fun*? You're a lunatic. And you know what? Maybe I'm a little crazy myself, because I'm fifteen and I want nothing more than to bash *your* head in with this mace." She swung her weapon at him, but it was deflected just before it hit. "Damnit!" She shouted, swinging again and again at his smirking face until she became too exhausted continue. She dropped her mace to the ground and collapsed back into her chair. "I will kill you," she vowed. "If not today, then tomorrow, or the day after."

"Oh child," the wizard sneered. "I thought that maybe at the end of all of this you would come to understand and appreciate all that I have done for you. But alas, not only do you fail to show any gratitude, you have the temerity to threaten me. Of all your friends you, little *priestess*, are the weakest. One by one your far stronger companions have fallen, leaving only you." He stood from his chair and towered over where she sat. As he spoke his voice got progressively louder. "Did you hear nothing of what I told you? Did you not see how easily I swatted away your wizard friend? Do you think I couldn't do the same to you? To anyone?" He raised his arms in triumph and shouted, "I am the ruler of the Arcanum, and soon the entire world. Nothing short of a god could stop me!"

Allison, the slightest glimmer of hope in her eyes, asked quietly, "How about a goddess?" The healing energy that she had failed to channel to Chuck still churned within her. It was more energy than she had ever held before, and more than she ever thought was possible. All at once she released it, not in a burst of healing, but in a Smite, the spell that the boys had heckled her for taking all those months ago. Warmth enveloped her, and with it came a sense of parental pride. The last thing she saw was Magnus' look of surprise as the power and fury of the goddess burst out of her, incinerating everything in the room.

CHAPTER 28

"Allison? Allie!"

The boy's voice drifted on the wind, stirring her from her stupor. It was dark, and Allison could just make out stars between the leaves on the trees above her. Her eyes watered and her body ached; when she pushed herself into a sitting position her elbow nearly gave out. Her mouth was dry and tasted of ozone. "Hrrrgh," she replied.

Lights flashed through the woods, and she heard more voices calling her name. She tried to reply again, "Hello?" but it turned into a fit of coughing. She heard footsteps approaching at a run and she turned to see a figure running toward her, a flashlight shining in her face.

"Allie! Thank god, it's you!" The boy crouched down next to her and smoothed the hair out of her face. "I found her!" he shouted, and his call was echoed from other voices in the distance. In the dim light she could just make out the features of the newcomer.

"S—Simon?" She rubbed her eyes with dirt-crusted hands, doing nothing to clear the moisture from her vision.

"Yeah, it's me. Where have you been? We've been looking for you all night! It's almost three AM!"

Rather than replying to his question, she threw her arms around him and held on for all she was worth, only letting go when someone draped a shiny blanket over her shoulders and a pleasantly scented man lifted her into his arms. She relaxed into his grasp and let herself nod off.

When she woke next, she was being carried into the lodge where the adventure had all begun. A large fire burned in the hearth, casting heat and a cheery glow throughout the room. The "tavern's" tables were turned into makeshift beds, and TJ, Chuck, and Jimmy all lay snoozing on them, covered in the same shock blankets that she had about her shoulders. Stu, who was seated at a nearby table, bounded across the room grinning like an idiot.

"I'm so glad you're safe. We were all so worried." He tried to give her a hug, but the EMT shooed him away.

"Don't crowd her. We need to check her out." He lay her down on an empty table and removed the stethoscope from around his neck. Seeing the man's puzzled look, Stu pointed out the clasps that held Allison's breastplate it together. Once it was off, the EMT gave her a quick once over, checking her heart, her breathing and her pupils.

The door burst back open and the room was suddenly crowded with bodies. "You found her?" Allison's mom cried out as she ran to her daughter's side, Allison's father in tow. The other kids' parents, along with a half dozen sheriff's deputies, several other EMTs, and others who had volunteered to search poured into the room. The noise woke the other boys from their sleep, and soon everyone was up and talking at once, focused on Allie, the last to be found.

Simon, the blue paint almost entirely washed off his face, asked, "What happened to you, Allie? We got separated in the woods and I totally lost track of you guys. None of the others can remember a thing after that."

"I...," she began, her eyes tearing up at the sight of her friend. "There were the bandits, don't you remember?" She looked to Stu for confirmation that what had happened to them was real.

"You mean the wolf men?" Simon persisted? "We fought some of those not long after we started." He looked over to where one of the game masters sat, a relieved look on his face. "Those *were* wolf men, right, Ewan?"

The other man nodded. "Yep. Well, sorta. We had a bandit ambush set up, but your group never got there."

From across the room TJ spoke for the first time. "Yeah, I'm sure that's what she means, Simon. It was those wolfmen." He held Allison's eyes as he added, "I don't remember any bandit ambush either. Isn't that right, Stu?"

Stu placed a hand on Allison's shoulder, gave it a squeeze, and grunted agreement. When she met his gaze he gave his head the tiniest shake. "Yeah. What he said."

She nodded, understanding his message. Her friends all looked exactly as they had at the beginning of the journey, with any hint of the physical changes they had experienced completely gone. Their eyes, however, told a different story, one that had been months in the making, with no happy endings for any of them.

"I ... I don't know, Simon. I must have hit my head or something, because I don't remember much. I guess it was some wolf men, right? And that little goblin guy who gave me the ring." She absently rubbed her ring finger with her thumb and was saddened to discover that the jewel was no longer there. She shook her head. "That's all I've got, I'm sorry."

"Well it's okay now honey," cooed her mother. "You're here and safe now and that's all that matters."

"Yeah," Allison replied, and dropped back into sleep.

EPILOGUE

"Hey, Bob, thanks for coming." The speaker, a heavyset man in his mid-twenties rose from where he sat at a table at the TGI Fridays in Springfield, Massachusetts. He extended a hand to the newcomer, who hesitated a moment before taking it and giving it a brief shake. The pair sat and the man continued, "I just put in an order for wings. You want a beer?" He gestured to his half-empty glass and made to flag down the server.

"No, I'm good, Ewan," Bob replied. "I've got another meeting to get to, so can't stay long." His voice sounded tired, and there were deep bags beneath his eyes, suggesting that he hadn't gotten much sleep in the last several weeks. It was six PM on a Friday night, and Ewan knew his friend was lying about the other meeting, but didn't push.

"Okay, that's cool. I've got a lot I'd like to bounce off of you,"— he gestured to a stack of papers to his left—"but we can catch up with that later. How are you holding up?"

"Not well." Bob ran a hand through hair that seemed to have grayed overnight. "Losing those kids scared the crap out of me, y'know? And even though none of their parents have even mentioned legal action, the idea is still keeping me up at night. That's what comes from being a lawyer and such."

"They signed waivers," Ewan began but his friend waved his hand dismissively.

"Oh, those don't hold up in court." He sighed. "But that's not the only thing. It's been," he began, then paused a few seconds before concluding, "a rough go."

Ewan reached across and patted Bob's arm comfortingly in an attempt to conceal his confusion over the other man's state. The organization had insurance, his friend had insurance, and as he had said, he was himself a lawyer. This was a total overreaction. "Well, okay. How about you go home and get some rest, and we can talk about this later? The gaming season is all done for the year anyway, so me and the other guys have got plenty of time to plan. I just wanted to know if you'd still be interested in letting us use your land next year.

Bob stood up, his face showing relief that he was being given an out from the meeting. "Thanks, Ewan. I may just do that," he said and turned to leave. He paused and turned back to the table. "Let me talk it over with my own attorney. If she gives it the green light, I'll feel a lot more comfortable about your using my place again."

"What about reprising your role as Magnus? The guys all agree that as far as evil overlords go, you were pretty great."

Yeah, about that," he took a deep breath before concluding, "I don't want to be the villain again this season. Do whatever you have to do with the plot—retcon it if you need to, but I just don't have the stomach to be evil, even if it's just fun and games."

He turned and left without another word. Ewan watched him go until a brightly clad waiter with far too many buttons on his suspenders blocked his view. As the man placed the plate of buffalo wings on the table he asked, "Another beer, sir?"

"No thanks," Ewan replied. My dinner meeting got cancelled, so I'm just gonna head out. Can I get the check?"

"So, you say it's going to be fun?" Allison smiled at TJ, who greeted her at his front door. "I've got pretty high standards for fun, I'll have you know."

"You bet, Allie," her best friend replied, showing her in and offering to take the backpack slung across her shoulder. "The whole gang is here and can't wait to play. Well, almost the whole gang, that is." Simon had returned to the football team and because it was nearing playoffs time his ability to play any games that didn't involve cleats and helmets was pretty much nonexistent. None of the others said it aloud, they all preferred it that way. He had no memory of what they'd been through, which was probably a blessing. He said he lost track of them when the group left the road the first time, and just went back to the lodge to wait. When the other groups came back in he knew something was wrong and the organizers called the police. Allison let TJ take her bag, and together they went to the dining room.

Around the table sat her friends, all of whom had become far closer to each other in the weeks since their 'adventure' as they referred to it. There was no evidence of any of their

LARP gear—hoodies and jeans were the late fall dress code for western Massachusetts, after all. The three boys waved at her as she walked in, and Chuck called out, "Ready to roll some dice, Allie?"

"You bet I am," she agreed. The others cheered at her enthusiasm. "And I came prepared!" She took her pack back from TJ's outstretched hand and drew a large box out from it. "First off, though—I call the dog."

"Dibs on the racecar!" shouted Stu and as the boys argued over who would get which piece, Allison unpacked the Monopoly board and handed out starting cash.

ACKNOWLEDGMENTS

These sorts of things really do take a village. My family continues to humor my writing, editing, and publishing. My friends cheer me on, buy my books, and cheerfully leave reviews online. My colleagues tout me in front of visitors to the Maine Business School with exclamations of, "You know … Dave is an author!" I am surrounded by people who support me unreservedly, and I love you all.

Once again Karen Lucky painted a gorgeous cover, and Alyssa did yeoman's work turning clunky prose into what you find here. Thank you, ladies.

One last time I'd like to say thanks to the entire NaNoWriMo community, including Chris Baty. Who would have thought that a short NPR interview broadcast through my shower speaker would have had such an impact on my life. It's now eleven novels later, and once again I'm diving into another month of frantic writing. Find me on the NaNo site at llabak. I love new writing buddies.

Did you like *No More Games*? The best complements you offer an author to is recommend them to a friend and to leave reviews online. It's almost as good as a hug.

ABOUT THE AUTHOR

Dave Barrett lives with his wife, three children, and an active imagination in Hampden, Maine, where he teaches financial accounting at the University of Maine. His first novel, *It's All Fun and Games*, was selected as a winner of the inaugural Nerdist Collection Contest. He's tickled pink to have brought the Fun and Games series to a conclusion.